GIRL, ERASED

(An Ella Dark FBI Suspense Thriller —Book Six)

BLAKE PIERCE

Blake Pierce

Blake Pierce is the USA Today bestselling author of the RILEY PAGE mystery series, which includes seventeen books. Blake Pierce is also the author of the MACKENZIE WHITE mystery series, comprising fourteen books; of the AVERY BLACK mystery series, comprising six books; of the KERI LOCKE mystery series, comprising five books; of the MAKING OF RILEY PAIGE mystery series, comprising six books; of the KATE WISE mystery series, comprising seven books; of the CHLOE FINE psychological suspense mystery, comprising six books; of the JESSE HUNT psychological suspense thriller series, comprising twenty four books; of the AU PAIR psychological suspense thriller series, comprising three books; of the ZOE PRIME mystery series, comprising six books; of the ADELE SHARP mystery series, comprising fifteen books, of the EUROPEAN VOYAGE cozy mystery series, comprising four books; of the new LAURA FROST FBI suspense thriller, comprising nine books (and counting); of the new ELLA DARK FBI suspense thriller, comprising eleven books (and counting); of the A YEAR IN EUROPE cozy mystery series, comprising nine books, of the AVA GOLD mystery series, comprising six books (and counting); of the RACHEL GIFT mystery series, comprising six books (and counting); of the VALERIE LAW mystery series, comprising three books (and counting); and of the PAIGE KING mystery series, comprising three books (and counting).

An avid reader and lifelong fan of the mystery and thriller genres, Blake loves to hear from you, so please feel free to visit www.blakepierceauthor.com to learn more and stay in touch.

BOOKS BY BLAKE PIERCE

PAIGE KING MYSTERY SERIES
THE GIRL HE PINED (Book #1)
THE GIRL HE CHOSE (Book #2)
THE GIRL HE TOOK (Book #3)

VALERIE LAW MYSTERY SERIES
NO MERCY (Book #1)
NO PITY (Book #2)
NO FEAR (Book #3

RACHEL GIFT MYSTERY SERIES
HER LAST WISH (Book #1)
HER LAST CHANCE (Book #2)
HER LAST HOPE (Book #3)
HER LAST FEAR (Book #4)
HER LAST CHOICE (Book #5)
HER LAST BREATH (Book #6)

AVA GOLD MYSTERY SERIES
CITY OF PREY (Book #1)
CITY OF FEAR (Book #2)
CITY OF BONES (Book #3)
CITY OF GHOSTS (Book #4)
CITY OF DEATH (Book #5)
CITY OF VICE (Book #6)

A YEAR IN EUROPE
A MURDER IN PARIS (Book #1)
DEATH IN FLORENCE (Book #2)
VENGEANCE IN VIENNA (Book #3)
A FATALITY IN SPAIN (Book #4)

ELLA DARK FBI SUSPENSE THRILLER
GIRL, ALONE (Book #1)
GIRL, TAKEN (Book #2)
GIRL, HUNTED (Book #3)
GIRL, SILENCED (Book #4)

GIRL, VANISHED (Book 5)
GIRL ERASED (Book #6)
GIRL, FORSAKEN (Book #7)
GIRL, TRAPPED (Book #8)
GIRL, EXPENDABLE (Book #9)
GIRL, ESCAPED (Book #10)
GIRL, HIS (Book #11)

LAURA FROST FBI SUSPENSE THRILLER
ALREADY GONE (Book #1)
ALREADY SEEN (Book #2)
ALREADY TRAPPED (Book #3)
ALREADY MISSING (Book #4)
ALREADY DEAD (Book #5)
ALREADY TAKEN (Book #6)
ALREADY CHOSEN (Book #7)
ALREADY LOST (Book #8)
ALREADY HIS (Book #9)

EUROPEAN VOYAGE COZY MYSTERY SERIES
MURDER (AND BAKLAVA) (Book #1)
DEATH (AND APPLE STRUDEL) (Book #2)
CRIME (AND LAGER) (Book #3)
MISFORTUNE (AND GOUDA) (Book #4)
CALAMITY (AND A DANISH) (Book #5)
MAYHEM (AND HERRING) (Book #6)

ADELE SHARP MYSTERY SERIES
LEFT TO DIE (Book #1)
LEFT TO RUN (Book #2)
LEFT TO HIDE (Book #3)
LEFT TO KILL (Book #4)
LEFT TO MURDER (Book #5)
LEFT TO ENVY (Book #6)
LEFT TO LAPSE (Book #7)
LEFT TO VANISH (Book #8)
LEFT TO HUNT (Book #9)
LEFT TO FEAR (Book #10)
LEFT TO PREY (Book #11)
LEFT TO LURE (Book #12)
LEFT TO CRAVE (Book #13)
LEFT TO LOATHE (Book #14)
LEFT TO HARM (Book #15)

THE AU PAIR SERIES

TINTED WINDOWS (Book #6)

KATE WISE MYSTERY SERIES
IF SHE KNEW (Book #1)
IF SHE SAW (Book #2)
IF SHE RAN (Book #3)
IF SHE HID (Book #4)
IF SHE FLED (Book #5)
IF SHE FEARED (Book #6)
IF SHE HEARD (Book #7)

THE MAKING OF RILEY PAIGE SERIES
WATCHING (Book #1)
WAITING (Book #2)
LURING (Book #3)
TAKING (Book #4)
STALKING (Book #5)
KILLING (Book #6)

RILEY PAIGE MYSTERY SERIES
ONCE GONE (Book #1)
ONCE TAKEN (Book #2)
ONCE CRAVED (Book #3)
ONCE LURED (Book #4)
ONCE HUNTED (Book #5)
ONCE PINED (Book #6)
ONCE FORSAKEN (Book #7)
ONCE COLD (Book #8)
ONCE STALKED (Book #9)
ONCE LOST (Book #10)
ONCE BURIED (Book #11)
ONCE BOUND (Book #12)
ONCE TRAPPED (Book #13)
ONCE DORMANT (Book #14)
ONCE SHUNNED (Book #15)
ONCE MISSED (Book #16)
ONCE CHOSEN (Book #17)

MACKENZIE WHITE MYSTERY SERIES
BEFORE HE KILLS (Book #1)
BEFORE HE SEES (Book #2)
BEFORE HE COVETS (Book #3)
BEFORE HE TAKES (Book #4)
BEFORE HE NEEDS (Book #5)
BEFORE HE FEELS (Book #6)

PROLOGUE

James Floyd waved goodbye to the receptionist and slipped out into the staff parking lot before any late-stayers could collar him. It was a mild night, a welcome change. The heating in his office had broken a few weeks ago, so he'd resorted to using a portable radiator that could barely heat a tent. Not ideal for the bitter night shifts, especially after the week he was having.

He remembered back to his first day on the job, 22 years ago by his napkin math. The head doctor had told him that the most essential part of the medical specialist's repertoire was cold detachment. Some people had it naturally; some people learned over time. And those that didn't acquire the skill had short and traumatic careers.

James quickly learned just how true this statement had been. He had peers who could deliver bad news like a weather report and not think twice about it. He envied them greatly, because with every piece of bad news he delivered, the guilt chipped away at his being a little bit more. This week brought more heavy burden than usual: a cancer diagnosis to a young dad, early signs of muscular dystrophy to a boy of 10, onset of dementia in a recently retired veteran.

And of course, Gladys, a new patient he'd become unprofessionally close to since last Monday. She'd come in complaining of back ache and ended up under the knife the next day. Gladys had been suffering from extreme kyphosis for well over a decade, but never got herself checked out because she *didn't want to cause a fuss.* Tough as old boots, but such attitudes didn't translate well to healthy lives, particularly for the elderly. James found himself wishing for the woman's recovery, maybe because she reminded him of his mother so much.

James pushed the button to unlock his car and the headlights flashed. His sedan was one of three in the parking lot. He checked his watch. Just after midnight. He didn't realize he'd stayed so late.

His foot caught something, invisible in the darkness. He stepped back and noticed a wooden board strewn on the floor. As he surveyed the lot, he noticed more of the same. Then he realized it was the debris left behind by the protesters from earlier in the day.

1

It was a new trend, maybe some Internet thing, James thought. Since the new laws came in, it was happening at hospitals up and down the country. Condensed down, it was basically activists campaigning against modern medicine. James had no time for such foolishness, especially as these people usually held extreme religious values too. They blindly believed in an invisible, all-knowing deity, but believing in a drug that killed bacteria was too much for them. It was silliness, misplaced delusion.

What usually happened was that these protesters kicked up a fuss, got their faces on the news, then disappeared once they'd had their fifteen minutes. It was nothing to worry too much about. James picked up the sign at his feet, folded it down, and took it to the trash can. Besides, judging by this person's grammar, these protesters weren't the sharpest tools in the shed.

AGAINST GODS WILL.

No apostrophe. Slanted writing. Yellow text on a brown background. It wasn't exactly a declaration of aptitude.

"You," someone shouted. "Don't go anywhere."

The sudden voice startled him. At this hour, the parking lot was always deserted. He spun around, looking for the source of the sound. A slovenly man waded out of the shadows. Overgrown beard. Bad skin. Small glasses on a round face. James didn't recognize him.

"Hello?" James said.

"Work here?" the man asked.

James edged towards his vehicle. "Yes. Do you?"

The stranger flapped his finger at the doctor. "It's not right, what you're doing."

"Excuse me?" *A straggling protestor,* James sighed to himself. Why was this man still here after midnight?

"You know what I mean. Don't play dumb."

James had no time for this. He didn't even have the energy to feel angry at him. All he felt was pity.

"Please, go home. You shouldn't be in this area of the hospital if you're not a staff member."

The stranger dropped back into the shadows but kept his glare on the doctor. James gripped his car's door handle while he waited for the man to disappear. James decided to notify security once he'd driven round the front of the building.

He pulled open the car door and stepped one foot inside, then froze before he could move any further.

2

A loud noise, maybe glass smashing? Then the stranger's voice again. James flirted with the idea of just driving off and leaving this for someone else to sort out, but what if this maniac had cornered another member of the staff? Maybe one of the admin girls? Or anyone who wasn't six-foot-two and 200 pounds like him?

He shut the car door and went to inspect. He moved across the barren parking lot, treading lightly. He parted some bushes and peered through to the other side, seeing the designated route for ambulances and nothing else. No straggling protestors, no midnight smokers. The stranger must have taken off in a hurry, maybe because he knew he was trespassing, and that wasn't a good look for his cause.

James stood still and heard the sounds of the night, broken by the thud of his beating heart. He heard the hum of distant traffic. A few chirping critters in the sparse woodland on the hospital's perimeter. He'd had plenty of altercations with patients and drifters over the years, but something about this guy sent a chill from head to toe; perhaps it was the late hour combined with the man's unexpected presence. He returned to the parking lot and headed towards his vehicle, keeping his wits about him. He didn't trust the man not to return and try something foolish.

James decided enough was enough for one week. Right now the prospect of a long bath with a good book was better than confronting deluded activists with their flavor-of-the-month objections.

Then his feet left the ground.

James flew back into the bushes, thorns piercing his skin. He scrambled for leverage but found nothing but brittle twigs. Before he could process what was happening, there was a foot buried in his chest. James gasped for air, kicking his feet at his invisible attacker. He tried calling for help but couldn't find his voice.

Then the attacker made himself known. A figure in black, camouflaged against the night. James's vision blurred to a fog. The man's outline twisted and melted against the dark, obscuring his face from James's view. There was something alarmingly familiar about him, but the oncoming shock clouded any chance of rational thought.

James coughed and spluttered up phlegm, then felt his body go into shock. With a hand around James's neck, this faceless man plunged a knife deep into his abdomen.

Blood erupted like a fountain, dyeing the green bushes crimson red.

James felt all determination fading. He couldn't move, only witness his own demise in a state of paralysis. He rolled onto his front and saw

3

the hospital, maybe for the last time. Through the bushes, only fifty feet away, paramedics loaded themselves into a waiting ambulance.

James tried to call out, reach out. He was voiceless. Help was visible but beyond his grasp.

This midnight attacker rolled the doctor onto his back then pulled something from his jacket.

The doctor recognized it. He'd seen it many times over his long career, but it never looked so ominous as it did now.

Suddenly, he found his voice, but his screams were drowned out by the blaring ambulance siren behind them.

CHAPTER ONE

Ella Dark took a seat on the crème sofa, feeling like this was all a hallucination. She was here, in a place she thought she'd never be, reeling from knife wounds and enough mental anguish to sink a ship. Only a few hours ago, she'd been in Delaware, hunting a predator who placed coins in people's eyes. Now she was in some rural farmland in Washington, far away from civilization, sitting beside the one person she believed could save her.

She scanned the front room, surprised at her ex-partner's exquisite tastes. Two large paintings adorned the walls with a gigantic TV between them. Ella noticed the remote controls were lodged beneath it. Mia always mentioned how much she hated television. In front of her, two tumblers sat on a glass coffee table.

"I'm sorry, do you have visitors?" Ella asked.

Mia Ripley sat beside her, cloaked in a satin robe, her expression betraying her feelings. Mia's red hair was pulled back in a bun. Ella saw some grays at the roots. It was very unlike Mia to be lax on the dye jobs.

"No. It's just easier to drink two at once. Call it self-regulation."

The last time they'd spoken, Mia had given up the drinking. "I thought you were off alcohol now?" Ella asked.

"Easier said than done. Do you want one?"

Ella felt a massive surge of relief. Before she stepped in here, she was worried Mia was going to fly off the handle, or just tell her exactly how much of a fool she'd been over the past few months. Ella wasn't sure why, but Mia seemed to genuinely want to talk to her. It was a comfort she couldn't find anywhere else in her life at the moment.

"No thank you. I need to think straight."

"Suit yourself," said Mia as she grabbed one of the tumblers. She swirled the glass and sat upright in her chair. Mia turned to Ella and raised her eyebrows. "I'm waiting."

"Waiting?"

"For you to tell me everything. You came to me. Why?"

Ella wasn't sure where to start, but she was grateful that Mia was at least allowing her to speak. For the past two weeks, Mia had dodged every call, email, and text message Ella had sent. She rubbed her eyes with her fingertips as she traced back recent events. She had a lot she wanted to talk about, but one question burned brighter than the others.

"Ripley, why have you let me in?" she asked.

Mia gulped her whiskey then wiped her lips. "Because I've had time to think."

"And?"

"You made a mistake. Well, several mistakes. But I can't hold it against you forever. Grudges just drag you down and I don't want that."

Now, it felt more like a hallucination than ever. Even Mia's tone felt off. Ella rubbed the bruise on her cheek just to feel the sting. This was definitely all real.

"What changed?" Ella asked.

"Nothing. I just needed time to process it. It's a lot for me to take in. Now, like I said, tell me everything."

"He's escaped," Ella blurted out. That was all she managed to say. Theories and worries hung loosely on her tongue but she kept them quiet. Ella needed to know what Ripley thought of the situation.

"Yes he has," said Mia. She put down her drink, sat back and looked towards her front door. Probably checking to see if she'd locked it, Ella thought. That meant Mia was worried for her own safety. Not a good sign.

"Do you know how?"

"No. The director called me earlier. That was all he told me."

"Same," Mia sighed. "It only happened a few hours ago so we'll know more soon."

Earlier in the evening, infamous serial killer Tobias Campbell had somehow escaped from his maximum security prison cell. The man who'd been imprisoned in an underground cage for nearly two decades had miraculously risen to the surface. It was Mia who'd originally caught Tobias 16 years before, and Ella who'd rattled the cage and incited the monster within. Ella's actions had been the reason why Mia had shunned Ella from her life, dropping her and requesting a new partner when she uncovered Ella's deceit.

Ella didn't want to say it, and by the looks of it, neither did her ex-partner.

"Dark, listen to me," Mia continued. "You know what this means, right?"

Ella nodded. She knew exactly what it meant.

"It means that me and you, we're not safe anywhere. Tobias has eyes and ears all over this country. He has links to criminal groups, underground sex rings, even the police and FBI. Before we caught him, we knew about his activities for years beforehand, but we could never catch up with him. He was always ahead, and now will be no different."

Ella acknowledged it but she wasn't so sure. "But how? He's much older, less able to move freely. We know his face. He's been in prison for 16 years, so surely his connections will have died out? Someone must recognize him if he's on the run?"

"Don't be so naïve, Dark. Tobias has been running his operations from behind bars all this time. All he needs to do is find a place to hide and he's as good as invisible. But with that said, I don't think he's planning on hiding out."

Sweat began to form on Ella's brow, despite the low temperature. "You don't?"

"Absolutely not. Tobias wouldn't break out of confinement just to sit in confinement again. You know what I mean, yes?"

She did. "He's coming for me."

"No, he's coming for *us*, and he wants to be the one who kills us. Tobias won't leave this to one of his lackeys. He's been dreaming of this for decades."

Her worst nightmare come to life. She'd met with Tobias twice and both times there'd been iron bars between them. Even so, she still felt vulnerable, and now all barriers had been removed. She was easy prey for one of the most sadistic serial killers in American history.

Ella took a moment to relive the events of the past few weeks. "When we were in Baltimore on the sex worker case, there was something else I never told you."

Mia's expression changed in light that there might be more secrets her ex-partner hadn't divulged. "I'm listening."

"People were watching me. I know, I sound paranoid. But I felt eyes on me constantly. Someone even slipped past me and said *Ella April Dark* to me. No one knows my middle name. No one except Tobias."

Mia exhaled and rested her hands behind her head. "I believe you. One hundred percent."

"You do?"

"Before we first caught Tobias, he used to do the same to my old partner twenty years ago. It's a game to him. Tobias isn't just content with murder. He's hell bent on crippling his victims mentally. This is his way of breaking you down and putting you on edge. It makes you more compliant to his demands. I'm guessing you visited him after our time in Baltimore?"

7

"Yes, the next few days."

"See. He motivated you through fear. He hasn't changed."

"But what does he want with me? I complied with his requests. I was the first person to visit him in years. Why would he want to kill me?"

Mia downed the rest of her whiskey. "Several reasons. First of all, you let him in. Secondly, you represent everything he hates. Authority, social order. Thirdly, you're connected to me. He sees himself as a genius and you as an underling trying to learn from him. He doesn't like that. But really, there's only one way this ends."

"We find him before he finds us," Ella confirmed.

Mia shook her head. "No. We kill him before he kills us."

Ella regretted not accepting Mia's offer of a drink. "Are you serious?"

"Deadly serious," said Mia.

Ella stared off into space for a moment, fighting against a jumble of heavy emotions. How many times had she found herself in the heat of the moment, face-to-face with an unsub, her finger itching on the trigger? Even in those moments, she'd never pulled the trigger and ended a life. Tobias was a monster, no doubt, but her hands trembled violently at the thought of seeking him out to end his life.

"Ripley, that's...," Ella rubbed her temples. "I don't even know what to say. It's crazy."

"Dark, I've been dealing with his bullshit for 16 years. Gifts to my door every year. Seeing his wiry face in the news. Not to mention the trauma he put me through. I've had just about enough. Edis will have every police department in the country on high alert, but..."

"But?" Ella asked. Mia's reasons were comprehensible. Tobias had been a poisonous thorn in her side for decades, and it was understandable she'd want to finally pull it out.

Mia bit her lip. "This is just between me and you. Off the record. Partner to partner. Okay?"

Partner. Ella had never been so overjoyed to hear that word. Was Mia accepting her back? Ella gestured that she was zipping her mouth shut, but still didn't like the direction of the conversation.

"The moment you see Tobias, and you will, shoot him down in flames. No talking. No arrests. No interrogation. Just empty your Glock right into his head. Paint the walls with his brains. Stamp his corpse to dust. Am I clear?"

"Ripley," Ella began. "I can't..."

"Why not?" Mia interrupted. "What's stopping you? Tobias has toyed with you as much as he has with me. I guarantee that he has plans for us, and Tobias's plans rarely involve instant death. He manipulates and torments. Do you want that in your future? Always looking over your shoulder?"

Two sides of the coin. There was no advantage to keeping Tobias alive. It would only bring more suffering to everyone, not just her and Mia. But was it their place to dispense such justice? Their job was to bring the wrongdoers to the courts. They weren't the iron fist. They weren't lords of life and death. They were agents of the law, with a license to kill providing it was absolutely justified.

Ella stared at her hands, imagining how she'd feel to actually fire rounds at him, fully aware that her actions would leave him six feet under. It would be a life-changing decision, something she'd have to take to her own grave.

But maybe it was justified.

An infamous serial killer, soon to be on the FBI's Most Wanted list, responsible for at least five murders and probably many more. Other than his criminal contacts, very few people wanted Tobias Campbell alive.

Perhaps, just this once, she could be an avatar for the world's true desires?

"But how would we explain it?" Ella asked.

"We don't. We say Tobias came for us, so we acted in self-defense. There isn't a jury in the world who would punish us for killing one of the world's most wanted."

Ella couldn't lie to herself. She saw the appeal, although she really didn't want to. But as appealing as it was, it was still a bad idea. If she and Mia actually went through with it, they'd be bonded by a deadly secret. Two could keep a secret if one of them was dead, the old saying went.

She pictured the scene in her head. Her and Tobias Campbell, face-to-face in an empty room.

God knows she'd fantasized about it enough times, but reality and fantasy were two very different things.

"Dark? What do you think? If we capture him alive, he's going straight back to prison to resume his criminal career. We'd basically revert back to how things were a few weeks ago. Nothing will have changed. Do you want that life?"

"No," Ella said. The truth was simple, plain as day. She didn't want Tobias Campbell alive. No more lies, even to herself. The cold reality of her situation was that Tobias Campbell had to die so she could live.

"You need to be fully on board, because if we do this, we'll be bonded by blood."

It was as if Mia had read her mind. As well as living with the fact she'd knowingly taken a life, she'd have to trust Mia with this fatal secret.

But there was no more ideal person to share such a secret with.

A selfish part of her wanted to be the one who pulled the trigger. For the torment Tobias put her through, delivering the lethal blow would be nothing short of poetic justice. But of course, Mia had just as many reasons too.

"Understood. I won't hesitate to take him down," Ella said. "I'm in. Bonded by blood."

"Good. You understand why we have to do this? Believe me, I've had 16 years of this nightmare, and I don't want you to endure even a fraction of it. It's been hell. Can I trust you with this?"

"You can trust me," Ella said. "No more lies, no more withholding information. If Tobias dies by our hands, my lips are sealed like a tomb. You have my word, on my father's grave."

"I believe you. Now, what else are we dealing with? How was your case in Delaware?" Mia asked.

"Up and down, but we got there in the end. They partnered me with Nigel Byford."

"Byford's a good guy. Not an expert on the criminal mind, though. How was he?"

"He was great, but all I could think was that if you were with me instead of him, we would have solved it in half the time," Ella said. "Did you get partnered with someone new?"

"Yes. Some airhead."

Ella was curious to hear the details, and a little jealous of this apparent airhead. "How did it go?"

"Terrible. She blew up a gas station."

Ella wasn't sure she heard it right. "She what?"

"Yeah. We caused about a hundred thousand dollars in damages so the director isn't my best friend right now."

Ella had a lot of questions. "How the hell did that happen?"

"Never mind that, what's important is that I realized how vital a good partner is. And all the while I was out there, I was worried about you. If you'd have ended up dead, I'd have felt responsible. Hell, I feel bad just looking at that bruise on your cheek."

Ella touched it and felt the sting again, but this bruise wasn't the work of the Delaware unsub. Her so-called boyfriend Mark had hit her once she'd gotten home, but something stopped her from revealing this little detail to Mia. Mia was very familiar with Mark, and she didn't want her to worry or feel responsible for it. Enough was going on already. She didn't want to drag Mia into her relationship issues too.

"Yeah, the unsub didn't go down easy. He stabbed me in the shoulder too, but I'll survive," Ella saw something in Mia's expression that resembled remorse, maybe guilt.

"Dammit, I wish I'd have been there," Mia said. "But from now on, I'm not going to let anything happen to you out there. If you're out in the field, I'm gonna be with you. Okay? If Tobias comes for one of us, he comes for both of us, capisce?"

Suddenly, the world felt like a much safer place. If there was one person she could trust with her life, it was the woman beside her. She'd already saved her life countless times since their first case, and since their biggest obstacle was still up ahead, Ella needed Mia more than ever.

"Thank you for forgiving me, Ripley. From now on, you can trust me. No more secrets."

The bruise on her cheek stung when Ella adjusted her jaw.

"Good. And I hope you can forgive me for overreacting. But in a way, this is good, because we can take down this monster for ourselves. It's given us an excuse to put an end to this chapter. And whatever happens, I promise I won't let anything happen to you."

"Thank you. Same here. We're stronger together."

"True. Now go home and rest. You look like you need it."

Ella prepared to take her leave. It was close to 1am, and she'd barely slept at all for the past few nights. Something told her she wouldn't get much sleep tonight either, despite her body crying out for respite. They headed to the door and Mia waved her off.

"Oh and Dark, one last thing," Mia called out.

Ella turned back.

"Lock your doors. Lock your windows. Cover your face. Keep a weapon on you. Don't give Tobias an opportunity, okay?"

Ella wouldn't. This time, she would be prepared.

CHAPTER TWO

Ella woke up the next morning with a searing pain in her shoulder and a dull ache on one side of her face. Now that her body had time to process the injuries, they'd settled into their final forms. She scrutinized them in the bathroom mirror, reassured that they were nothing serious. The laceration on her shoulder was already beginning to scar over and the bruise was already fading to a sickly yellow. It was nothing a touch of makeup couldn't fix.

It was Saturday so she didn't need to be in the office, but she had a lot of work planned. The previous week, Ella had discovered that in the days before her father's death, he'd taken out a loan from an underground association known as Red Diamond. The Diamonds were well-known throughout Virginia when Ella was a kid, and the hushed whispers around town were that every Diamond member had blades sewn into their boots. Apparently, you could always recognize a member by a diamond-shaped scar somewhere on their body.

Whenever someone in Virginia died under suspicious circumstances, locals would always joke that the Diamonds probably had something to do with it. How much of it was playground rumor and how much was true remained a mystery.

If her dad had borrowed money from them, chances are his finances were in the ground. That's why she'd liaised with his former bank for a copy of his bank records. Of course, her dad had passed away 25 years ago, and back then, a lot of transactions circumvented banks entirely. In the nineties, cash was king.

Ella armed herself with coffee and took a seat on her lounge floor. There was no sign of her roommate, but there never was on Saturday mornings. Probably stayed at one of her lovers' houses, Ella decided. The thought reminded her of her own so-called lover, or ex-lover after what he did last night. Mark Balzano was scheduled to begin investigating a new case today, so hopefully that would keep him from contacting her today. She knew he'd come crawling back around eventually, but she told herself to stay strong. There was no place in her life for domestic abuse, not to mention Mark's jealousy was completely irrational. Mark had problems and she wasn't prepared to fix them for him. He wasn't a child. He had to do that himself, and until he did, she wanted no part of him.

She picked up the receipt that she'd recently found in her father's possessions. A small, handwritten note on yellowed paper.

Ken, consider this your acknowledgment of borrowed monies. Must be repaid in full with ten percent interest by 05/25/95. OWA.

Ella had run the note through graphology software at the FBI headquarters. She'd printed out the results.

Name: Owen William Angels
Born: 05-31-1970
Occupation: Unknown
Address: Unknown
Prior Offenses: 13

Among the information was a request for planning permission for the Red Diamond Group. Ella had checked the location of the building but it had been long since demolished. A dead end, unless she could dig into the history of the owners. If these financial records didn't lead anywhere, that was her next step.

She began leafing through the pile of documents the bank had kindly printed out for her. They only went back to 1992 because that was as far as records were kept, but it meant she had three years' worth of documents to inspect. If her dad had debt problems, something in here would let her know.

January 1992. Her father's bank balance began at $14,000. Not bad considering he was a single father and manual laborer. Payments came and went in a discernible rhythm: gas, electricity, water, mortgage, phone charges. Each month, about $1500 went out and $2000 came in. There were a few withdrawals of a hundred dollars or so, but nothing that warranted suspicion.

The pattern continued until 1995; then, the total balance quickly dwindled. In fact, money was hemorrhaged out of the account at an alarming rate.

In January of that year, her dad had made multiple withdrawals of a thousand dollars, all in $200 bursts. Ella remembered that once upon a time, $200 was the maximum amount one could withdraw. This pattern carried on until May 1995, when the bank balance was completely demolished.

On May 2, 1995, her dad withdrew $11,000 in one lump sum. Not in instalments this time, which meant he'd gone into the bank and liaised with the teller. That was the only way someone could take out such a substantial amount of cash.

Then the transactions continued as normal but came to an abrupt stop at the end of the month. That was the same month Ella had discovered him dead in his bed.

She glared at the figure on the paper, as though staring at it for long enough would reveal the mystery behind it. Why would someone need $11,000 in cash? To pay a contractor? To purchase something extravagant?

No, there was no way Ken would have done that. Even in the nineties, no contractor would take such a large cash payment. And the idea of her dad buying something that expensive was even more unlikely. He was a simple man, frugal as it came. As long as he had clothes on his back and food on the table, he didn't care for anything else.

Or at least, that's how she remembered him. But this revelation that he may have had a gambling problem cast her memories in a whole new light. Was that the reason for these multiple $200 transactions? And possibly this large withdrawal too? Did Ken take a chance on a big win? Or maybe he was just trying to pay back the cash he'd borrowed from this seedy Red Diamond group?

But if this was true, there was nowhere else to go. She couldn't trace cash transactions, so this route was a dead end. She'd have to dig more into the Red Diamond group, or try and trace this mysterious Owen Angels.

Ella picked herself up and peered out onto the balcony. It was a bright morning, but Ella wasn't quite ready to bask in the new sun just yet. She didn't want to head out where she was visible, because any hidden corner could conceal a threat. The idle cars below, the space behind the communal trash cans. Tobias Campbell was now among the people. He could have eyes on her at any moment. Every shadow was a threat.

Even so, things felt a little clearer now that she and Mia had aired their troubles. She could muse on a subject without her thoughts constantly jumping to a different issue.

While she admired the view in the distance from the safety of the indoors, the parking lot gates slowly opened. A vehicle drove slowly onto the lot. A vehicle she recognized.

Ella took too long to clock the number plate. The driver looked out his window and saw her.

Oh, Christ, she said to herself as she rushed back inside and locked the door. She pulled the drapes shut, locked the windows.

But something told her it was too late.

CHAPTER THREE

Mia stood outside the office door of FBI Director William Edis. She usually just walked right in, but there was more than a little heat between them since Mia's trainee exploded a gas station on their first case. She didn't want to fan the flames by assuming their relationship was still stable.

"Come in," Edis called.

Mia entered and took a seat on the leather chair beside Edis's desk. The director kept his head in a pile of paperwork, then rattled his pen between his teeth. In the thirty years she'd known him, she'd never seen him look so haggard. He used to be a real handsome beast: devilish good looks on a muscular frame. Now he had a pale face, receding gray hair and that disarming smile he became famous for was long gone. He looked like stress incarnate, and Mia couldn't understand why he didn't just pack up and take his millions to a farm in Wyoming.

"Will, is everything alright?"

The director threw his pen on his desk. It rolled all the way off. "No, it's not. Things couldn't be worse."

"Talk to me. How can I help?"

"I don't even know where to start, Ripley."

"I've spoken to my old trainee. She's back behind a desk after the accident…"

"That's not important," Edis interrupted. "Damages are damages. No one died and that's all I care about."

Mia didn't expect such a dismissal of events. Tobias's escape clearly overshadowed the incident. "Agreed."

"We have two bigger problems to worry about. You know the first one."

"Tobias Campbell."

Edis stood up and looked out of the window behind his desk. He leaned against it with one hand. For a moment, Mia worried he was about to jump out.

"Yes, Tobias Campbell. He's out there right now. One of the biggest catches in FBI history, and he slipped back into society right under our noses. Needless to say, we're a laughing stock at the minute. This morning alone I've had the CIA and MOD on my case. I've got a call

15

with the vice president in an hour, and I really don't know what to tell her."

"Sir, with all due respect, his escape wasn't our fault. Surely it's the prison's responsibility?"

"No, it's ours. We could have made special arrangements to have him executed. We could have had stricter protocols around medical issues. We could have shipped him to Devil's Island and let him rot."

"Medical issues?" Mia asked. "Is that how he got out?"

"Yes. His pulse stopped beating so they transferred him to McLean Hospital in Maine. That's standard procedure for Maine State Prison."

Mia could already picture how the rest played out. She knew there'd have been bloodshed. Tobias wouldn't have had it any other way. "Isn't that a little naïve of them, sir? Taking one of the most dangerous serial killers in history *out* of prison?"

Edis returned to his desk and searched for his pen. He combed through the desk then quickly gave up. "They thought he was as good as dead. Less questions if a prisoner dies in a hospital and not in their cell, you see. But once he got to McLean, he miraculously came back to life. He killed two guards and a nurse in an elevator and then just walked out. The CCTV footage is… concerning."

"He's been planning that for a long time," Mia said. "An organized psychopath like Tobias would…"

Edis held up his palm. "Ripley, please. I don't need your psychobabble right now. What I need is Tobias Campbell back behind bars."

Or dead, she said to herself. "Agent Dark and I can get on the case immediately. If he hunts anyone, it will be her."

Edis waved both hands around. "No. Not a chance. You and Miss Dark are not to be involved at all, understand?"

Ripley had to stop herself from jumping out of her chair. The comment made her clench her fists. "What? Sir, you must be joking? We are the best chance we have of catching Tobias."

"I don't doubt it, but you're too close to this. I don't want you in Washington for the next few days, so I'm sending you both on assignment."

Mia couldn't believe it. She leaned forward and grabbed Edis's desk. "But sir, that's not a good…"

"Ripley." Another interruption. "I'm not debating this with you. You and Miss Dark are targets, and if one or both of you came to harm, that's another big loss for the Bureau, not to mention I'd be losing two of my top workers. Not going to happen, do I make myself clear?"

Mia dropped back in her seat. She hated to admit it, but Edis had a point. Still, the thought of someone else putting a bullet in Tobias's head filled her with a jealous rage. That was her kill to have, no one else's. The closest she'd get to vengeance was spitting on his grave, and that wasn't anywhere near enough for her.

But was safety more important? Especially Ella's safety? What was stopping Tobias from offing Ella while she was blissfully unaware? In her bed, in the grocery store, filling up her car? Tobias could easily sneak up on her and end her life in milliseconds. She wouldn't put it past him to do exactly that.

The previous night when Ella was at her place, Mia felt her partner traveling the same path she'd done as a younger agent. Growing jaded with the world, longing for justice that would never come. It took Mia years to come to terms with the cruel nature of this position, and those years were a storm of rage and frustration. She didn't want to see the same happen to the rookie.

"I get it, Will, but you of all people must understand how hard this is. That man nearly killed me, and there isn't a day that goes by where I don't dream of him being pulled apart by horses."

"And that's why you can't hunt him down now. You'll either end up killing him or getting so frustrated that it'll take years off your life. Take a step back from it all. We've alerted all state police in the country and every single precinct in Maine to find him. We have a dragnet and tips hotline already in place. If someone sees Tobias, we'll know about it immediately. We've got the world looking for him, and the world can do a lot more than you and Miss Dark."

Mia accepted it. Whatever route brought Tobias down was best. She had to put her own emotions aside since other people's lives were at stake here too. Tobias had been in solitary confinement for 16 years and there was zero chance his thirst for blood had died down. He was probably more violent than ever.

"Right, so what am I supposed to do? Go to Hawaii until Tobias is back behind bars?"

Edis searched through his papers and found a brown folder. He threw it into Mia's lap. "New Jersey," he said.

"What? New Jersey? You know I hate New Jersey."

"And I hate skiing but my wife still makes me go every year. I need you in New Jersey because we have a new case out there. It landed on my desk this morning, and it's just another problem on the pile. So if you really want to help me out, you and Miss Dark can work your magic. *And* you can hide away without having to look over your shoulder."

Mia ran her hand through her hair. The last place she wanted to be was New Jersey, but if there was a case to work on, she had an obligation to go. "Alright. Fill me in." She started leafing through the folder.

"Last night, a doctor was found murdered outside his hospital in Princeton. Stabbed and then strangled."

Mia found the first crime scene photograph. It showed a middle-aged man lying in a pile of dirt, eyes wide open in that familiar death stare. But the first thing that drew her attention was the foreign object sticking out of his mouth.

"What's that? Wire?" Mia asked.

"No. Bizarrely, it's a feeding tube. Our unsub stabbed our victim and then choked him with this tube. Very odd behavior, I'm sure you'll agree."

Doctor. Feeding tube. The connection was there already. Maybe a killer that had a vendetta against the medical community? A vengeful patient? Or maybe the tube was a weapon of opportunity?

"I'm guessing this isn't an isolated incident," Mia said.

"Correct. This is the second victim within a two-mile radius within the week. I haven't had time to read the case file in full yet, so you and Agent Dark will have to dissect it. I know it's Saturday, but I need you both to squash this one ASAP. We desperately need a win here. I'm sure you understand why."

Mia grabbed her bag and pulled out her car keys. "You can count on us, sir."

"I know, that's why I'm sending you on this and not anyone else. Call the admin department and have them arrange your flights out there. Get this one done and don't rush back home. Stay and enjoy New Jersey."

Mia had to stop herself from laughing. "Yeah, right. Will you call me as soon as you have any updates on Tobias?"

Edis went back to his paperwork. "Promise. By the time you get back, we'll have him in chains."

Doubtful, Mia thought. She took her leave out into the hallway. *Because I'm going to get him first.*

18

CHAPTER FOUR

Ella crouched down in her kitchen, as though that might somehow stop the inevitable from happening. She considered jumping over her balcony or climbing onto the roof of the apartment complex.

No, that was foolish, and pointless.

Knock, knock, knock.

Ella didn't want to see him, couldn't look at his face so soon. Anger balled up in her stomach, and she was afraid that if she heard his voice again, she'd do something she'd regret.

She waited it out. Her car was in the parking lot, but it didn't mean she had to be home.

Then she remembered he'd seen her on the balcony. *God dammit,* she said to herself.

Two more knocks, heavier this time. She had no choice. Time to face the music and put this guy in his place... for the second time in 12 hours.

Ella went to her front door and peered through the spy glass. It was him alright, with a smug expression on his face. Yes, she was pretty certain she was going to break his legs.

She yanked the door open with force. "Mark. What?" she asked.

Mark Balzano leaned against the door frame, a little too casually for Ella's liking. This man had struck her in the face only the night before, and he had the nerve to show himself so suddenly?

"Sorry for stopping by, I just wanted to see you," Mark said. He was wearing a brown jacket, white t-shirt and faded jeans. He had his hair tied up. Ella hated the sight of him.

"Stopping by? What the hell is wrong with you?"

"Woah, calm down, will you?" Mark strode back and held up his hands defensively. "I said I was sorry about last night, and I just wanted to prove it to you." He reached into his jacket and pulled something out. Ella scrutinized it with curious eyes.

"What's that?"

"You told me once you liked Guns 'N' Roses, didn't you?"

"Yeah, who doesn't?"

"I got this for you. It's signed by them." He passed the gift to Ella. It was the first Guns 'N' Roses album with black squiggles on the front.

"Vinyl?" Ella asked. "Have you lost your mind?"

"It's a collectible," Mark said. "I thought you'd be a little more pleased with it, to be honest."

Ella pushed the gift back into Mark's chest. He clutched it. "It's very thoughtful of you. The gift is very nice, and if you'd have given it to me before yesterday, I'd have been the happiest girl in the world. But Christ almighty Mark, you can't hit me one day and then bring me a vinyl the next. Is this supposed to make up for what you did?"

"Can we just talk?" Mark pleaded. "Come on. You owe me that much."

"Owe you? Mark, I'm one comment away from kicking the shit out of you. I don't owe you a damn thing. We went out, and now we don't. Deal with it."

Mark looked defeated and that was exactly how she wanted it. She'd fallen for his charm one too many times. *Fool me once,* she said to herself.

"Look, just five minutes. I just want to make sure you're doing okay."

Ella asked herself a series of questions. Would kicking him out turn him violent? Was he trying to worm his way back in by feigning affection? And would this affect their working relationship? After all, there was a chance they could be assigned to the same case in the future. Any bad blood between them would naturally overspill into their professional lives too.

"Five minutes," Ella said. "But this doesn't mean I forgive you." She stepped away from the door but didn't turn her back to Mark. If there was one thing she knew about him, he was unpredictable, prone to violent mood swings. His switch could flip at any moment.

Ella walked into the lounge and Mark followed, shutting the door quietly behind him.

"Dark in here," he said. "Who are you hiding from?"

Ella kept her distance. "You."

"I didn't mean it. I just acted out. I'm sorry."

"I'm not interested in excuses," said Ella. "Now, say what you have to and get out of here."

Mark took a seat on Ella's sofa, despite the lack of invitation. "How are your injuries?" he asked.

"Fine. No thanks to you."

Mark clasped his hands together and looked down at the floor. "I mean from your case."

"I got stabbed in the shoulder. How do you think they're doing?"

"Right. Sorry. How were things with your partner?"

That topic again. What was Mark's problem? "Good. He saved my life. I owe him one."

"I bet you do," Mark said. "You got along well, then?"

"As good as we needed to. Why do you care?"

"Because I was worried. How many times do I need to tell you?"

"Mark, I'm a grown woman. I can handle myself out there. I've taken down criminals without anyone else's help, okay?"

"Yeah. I know," Mark said as he rose to his feet. "But that's not what I'm talking about."

Ella stepped back towards the kitchen area. Just feeling Mark's body warmth was making her itch. She felt nothing but pity for him since he exploded in a jealous rage last week, and nothing but disgust since he laid his hands on her last night. "I'm not talking about this anymore. Because there's nothing to talk about."

Mark laughed. "Sounds like a guilty conscience."

Ella leaned against the counter, now realizing her fists were curled. "Mark, are you honestly worried that I was sleeping with someone else while I was out there? Why in God's name would I do that? Do you think I'm some horny teenager who can't keep her legs shut?"

"A woman. On her own. Out in the field. I've seen it happen."

Ella was sick of hearing it. These baseless accusations from an insecure mind. "What possibly suggested I'd do such a thing? You can't just assume that's what I'm like. Just because you've been with *other* women like that, doesn't mean we're all the same. You're a smart guy. How can you not understand this?"

Mark began to pace. "Right, so now I'm stupid? Ella, remember who saved your life a couple of weeks ago down in Baltimore. Me. Not anyone else. I was there for you."

"And I'm massively grateful for that. I'm indebted to you for that. But you must realize you've got a violent jealous streak and until you sort it out, no one will want to be with you. When I was on assignment, you texted me constantly, like a stalker. Not only that, but you made blind accusations without any proof. You came to a conclusion in your mind and mistook it for the truth. And when I confronted you about it, you hit me."

Mark stood in the center of the lounge, shoulders arched. A defensive stance, Ella realized.

"And I apologized. What more do you expect?"

"Yeah, you did apologize, but it was a step too far. That's why we're not together anymore."

The comment stirred something in her ex-boyfriend. She watched his expression morph into fury. "Not together? You want to throw this relationship away because of a small mistake?"

"A mistake?" Ella gasped. "Leaving your car unlocked in a mistake. Hitting your girlfriend is domestic violence. Please tell me you understand the difference." Ella had reached her limit. She just wanted this conversation over and this man gone from her apartment. Their professional relationship be damned. If it affected them in the workplace, so be it. She couldn't take any more of his manipulation.

Mark strode towards her, blocking off the kitchen exit. "You know this isn't over, right? We still have plenty of gas in the tank. You're not going to just abandon our relationship at the first sign of trouble."

Ella moved back and lay her hands on the kitchen surface. She gripped a rolling pin in one hand and had to use all of her willpower to not swing it at the man in front of her.

"I'm not abandoning anything. I'm breaking off something that needs to be broke. And you're not going to talk me out of it because you'll just end up doing the same thing to me again. You'll accuse me of cheating and hit me when I deny it."

Mark slammed one fist down on the kitchen counter with a sudden bang. Ella jumped back. She gripped the rolling pin harder and planned the next few moves out in her head. Mark had a size and strength advantage, but she'd taken down bigger people in the past. One well-placed move and she could be out of the apartment in seconds.

"Things will be different now. I was just having a hard time. You must understand how hard it's been for me recently? Confined to a desk, not able to do the job I love. It's really taken its toll."

"No excuses, Mark. Please, get out of here now. You've had your five minutes."

"I'm not finished," Mark snapped.

"Well I am."

Mark cornered her, came so close she could smell that familiar cologne. A scent she once favored but was now unspeakably ugly to her.

"You're not leaving me. You can never leave me, understand?" Mark said. He trapped her against the corner of the kitchen unit and put his hands on either side of her. He lowered his face up against hers as one of his arms slowly raised up.

Ella said nothing. She gripped the rolling pin handle so tight it began to hurt. Her muscles twitched with adrenaline and she prepared to take Mark out before he could do anything to her. At the moment of launch, a knock at the door interrupted their altercation. Neither person took their eyes off the other.

"Mind getting that?" Ella said, finally.

Mark blew hot air into her face. Then another knock came. Mark retreated and stumbled out into the hallway. Ella breathed a sigh of relief, glad that things didn't get physical. She heard Mark open the door, then heard clattering high heels make their way inside. Ella couldn't have been happier to see the new arrival.

"Ripley?" she asked. "What are you doing here?"

"Dark in here," she said. Mia glanced between Ella and Mark. "Sorry, not interrupting anything am I?"

"No. You're not," Mark said. "Look, I'm gonna get out of here. Mia, good to see you again. Ella, I'll see you soon."

She locked eyes with Mark and sighed heavily. His whole demeanor had transformed in the moments since Mia had arrived. Heated a minute ago, cool and calm now. It concerned Ella just how quickly he was able to shift gears.

"Okay," Ella said and left it at that. She didn't want to cause a scene in front of her resurrected partner. Mark left, closing the door quietly as he did.

"Everything okay? Pardon my intrusion," Mia said.

"It's fine." Ella shook her head. Her heart pounded so hard she was worried Mia might hear it. "We weren't in the middle of anything."

"I can see that. You still have your clothes on. Anyway, pack your bag because we're going to sunny New Jersey."

"What? Now?" Ella asked.

"Yes. Now. There's a serial case. We've got a guy killing medical staff. Are you in or out?"

Ella glanced at the pile of paperwork sitting on her lounge floor. She did plan on dedicating this weekend to investigating her father's murder, but if duty called then so be it. Besides, she could really use a distraction.

"Partners again?" Ella asked, the words trembling on her lips. She kept her composure, not letting her reactions to Mark overflow into her new conversation. The woman in front of her once told her to approach every new situation with a smile. Keep the past in the past.

"The old team. Just don't blow up any gas stations," Mia said.

"I make no promises," said Ella. "But what about Tobias? Shouldn't we make him our priority?"

"The director put his foot on down on that. Come on, I'll tell you on the way to the airport."

Regardless of the case, Ella was ready to hit the road again. And with Mia by her side, that was the best situation she could ask for. Maybe if she got out of D.C. for a while, she could plan the next few weeks without having to look over her shoulder every few minutes.

"Let me get my things. I'll be ready in two minutes," she said.

CHAPTER FIVE

Ella read through the new case file in the car. Mia was the designated driver. Their destination was the Reagan Washington National Airport.

Now that the adrenaline had worn off, Ella felt the effects of her confrontation with Mark. What did he mean, *he could never leave her?* She'd already made her feelings known, but that wasn't enough for him? He expected her to stay with him regardless of how he acted? As far as she was concerned, their connection was severed, and if Mark had a problem with that, he'd have her fists to answer to. She really didn't want it to come to that, because on the surface, Mark was an intelligent man who understood human emotion. Hell, it was part of his job. How could one person be so contradictory?

The case file trembled in her hands. She'd read the first few paragraphs but then her concentration had faltered. Ella caught Mia sneaking a few glances over at her.

"Everything okay, Dark? You usually zip through those files in seconds."

Ella picked herself up and focused. "Sorry. Just taking it all in." She read again from the start.

"So, victim number one was Leslie Buddington, 29 years old. Female. Found dead in her car outside Tower Lodge nursing home where she worked. Stabbed in the stomach and then asphyxiated."

"But that's not all. Look at the photos."

Ella turned a few pages and found the crime scene shots. The first picture showed a woman sitting in her driver's seat, head lolled back with something resembling a thin, red rope around her neck. The image sent her stomach in knots.

"Oh, Christ. What's this killer trying to say?"

"Keep reading," Mia said.

"Victim number two was James Floyd, 52-year-old male, found dead in the staff parking lot of Princeton Hospital. Same method of killing. Stabbing and then asphyxiation."

Mia veered onto the freeway and Ella watched the city pass by as she organized her thoughts. There was a tangible link between the victims, but nothing they could absolutely confirm. She checked out the crime scene photos of the second victim. The poor gentleman lay at the foot of a thorny bush, a pool of blood oozing from his abdomen. There was a red object lodged down his throat.

"Another medical tube?"

"Another medical tube. Strange signature, I'm sure you'll agree."

Two victims but vastly different victimology. A young woman and an older man. This fact alone was enough to arrive at several assumptions. On cue, Mia asked the question.

"What do you make of it?"

"If victim number one was found in her car, that meant he ambushed her there. He must have waited for her, then struck once she was inside," Ella said.

"I can't disagree."

"But victim number two must have been lured to this location, or he was placed there post-mortem. Slight variation in M.O."

"Or they got into a fight and it bled out somewhere else. Impossible to say right now."

"The link is that both of these victims worked in healthcare," Ella said. "Maybe someone with a vendetta against the medical industry?"

"Could be, but dig deeper."

Ella leafed through the crime scene photos. She put herself at the scene. Why these people? What did this killer want? What was he trying to say?

"The medical tubes add some weight to that theory, but given they were killed near places of medical aid, medical tubes could have been a weapon of convenience."

"You really think so?" Mia asked.

Ella did, but the comment suggested her partner didn't. "It's hard to say without knowing more. If we could gauge whether these exact tubes came from the particular establishments these victims worked at…"

"No," Mia said. "The medical tubes are everything. He's using them to send a message. Why would he leave the tubes at the scenes if he wasn't? Serial killers only leave evidence at a crime scene if their psychopathology compels them to. The tubes are a vital component of this killer's M.O. and we need to focus on them."

"Of course," Ella said. "I should have thought of that."

"Pretend you're our unsub. Why wouldn't you just remove the tubes as a forensic countermeasure?"

"Good point. And why would he bother to strangle them if he had a knife?"

"That's another thing we need to look at," Mia said. "Stabbing followed by strangulation tells us a lot about this offender."

Ella waited for Mia to continue but she didn't. Ella took the reins.

"It means he wants to feel a personal connection with them. Strangling is a very intimate way of killing someone."

"Correct. And what does this tell you about the physical traits of our unsub?" Mia asked. She swerved into the overtaking lane and crept up to 90mph.

Ella looked out at the passing scenery and cast her mind back to similar murderers in the past. What historical serial killers utilized similar approaches? John Wayne Gacy, Dennis Rader, Gary Ridgway, Samuel Little, the Danilovsky Maniac. What did they have in common?

"We can assume the unsub is male, and we can assume he's below average in physical ability."

"Why?" Mia asked.

"He stabbed them to subdue them. He's not confident in his ability to restrain them with strength or intimidation. That could suggest he's small, weak."

"I'd say you're thinking along the right lines. Why do you think he chose these victims?"

Ella inspected the crime scene locations. Both near empty lots. Both in places that would be deserted at night. "They were victims of opportunity," Ella said. "Both killed at night in isolated parking lots. These victims were in the wrong place at the wrong time."

"Possibly," Mia said, "but we can't know for sure until we dig deeper. They could very well have been purposely targeted, but my gut instinct tells me this unsub is targeting random members of the medical community. The care home that Leslie Buddington worked at was part of the same hospital network as Princeton. They exchange staff. The care home operates as a developmental ground for some of the trainees."

"So, maybe a disgruntled patient? Or a co-worker?"

"Both plausible ideas," Mia said, "but we can't say anything for sure until we know more. There's one other thing we need to consider too. What is it?"

Ella retraced the steps. She'd covered everything. Victimology. Methodology. Physical traits of the unsub. She was eager to remind Mia just how good of a partner she was, so she wracked her brain looking for the missing piece.

She reached the end of the case file.

Of course, she realized. What came after the second victim?

"Who's he going to target next?" Ella asked.

The Saturday morning traffic made the journey as short as it could possibly be. No commuters on their way to the office, so it was just early risers heading to the beach. Signs for the Reagan Washington National Airport came into view.

"Yes. Given this victimology, what's his next target going to be?"

The victims couldn't be any more different. A middle-aged male, a late-twenties female. Different body types, different locations, even different approaches when it came to his attacks. Predicting the next move was borderline impossible. Princeton likely had no shortage of medical personnel to target.

"Another member of the medical community," Ella said. "It's impossible to predict anything else."

"More or less. Given the disparity in victim type, we can conclude that these aren't sexually-motivated attacks. This unsub isn't a sadist. These kills mean something else entirely, and until we figure out what, we have no idea who he'll target next."

Ella put the case file in her bag and dwelled on the new information. She did her best to forget about Mark, about Tobias. At least for the time being. She had Mia beside her and if anyone could keep her safe, it was the top field agent in the FBI.

And from now on, no more secrets. That's what she told herself. She caught her reflection in the side mirror and saw the bruise on her cheek peeking through her makeup. She extended her jaw and felt the sting.

But now wasn't the time to tell Mia that one of her oldest colleagues was an abuser. That was a conversation for another time, if ever.

"When we get to New Jersey, we need to see the most recent crime scene," Mia said. "Figure out what this unsub is trying to say."

Ella couldn't wait. It was time to remind Mia what a valuable partner she was, and show that their teamwork could be the thing that finally brought down Tobias Campbell. Ella had been waiting for Mia to give her the latest on the subject but had remained quiet on it so far.

"What did the director say about Tobias?" Ella asked reluctantly.

"Not our responsibility," Mia said.

"What? You can't be serious?"

"That's what the director said. We're too close to the case. It's in someone else's hands right now."

Ella leaned her elbow against the door. Was this a good thing? Was she safer keeping a distance from Tobias?

"I'm not sure how I feel about that," she said.

"I hate it," said Mia. "If anyone should be assigned to finding Tobias, it's me and you. But the director calls the shots, so what are we supposed to do?"

Ella had a good idea of what they could do. "We could defy his order?" she suggested. As soon as the words left her mouth, she felt like she'd violated some unspoken rule. But she didn't regret it.

Mia grinned as they came off the freeway towards the airport parking lot. "Thirty years," Mia said.

"Thirty years?"

"That's how long I've answered to an FBI director, and in that time, I've never once said no. I've done everything they've asked and more. And you know, I understand where Edis is coming from here. We *are* too close to Tobias. We *would be* putting ourselves in danger by pursuing him."

Ella felt a swerve coming. "Absolutely. But we put ourselves in danger every week. Tobias or not."

"Exactly," Mia said. "And that's why I think, for the first time in thirty years, it's time to break the rules a little."

Ella clenched her fist in exhilaration. The idea was still anxiety-inducing, even after dwelling on it all night. Her stomach tied in knots at the thought of it.

But she had no choice.

"I'm in," she said.

CHAPTER SIX

Ella stood just outside the hospital parking lot and surveyed the crime scene while Mia fiddled about with something in the back of the cab. Yellow tape cordoned off the whole lot, and the usual parkers had been relegated to the street behind them, judging by the wall-to-wall vehicles. Up ahead, a group of police officers surrounded the spot where last night's murder had taken place.

She'd never been to New Jersey before, but it seemed like a hospitable place. It had been a swift hour-long flight and a half-hour taxi ride, but after the excessive traveling she'd done in the past few weeks, all these cities were starting to blur into one.

Mia joined her with her phone to her ear. She hung up. "What do you make of this scene?" she asked Ella.

"Not as isolated as I expected," Ella said. "Our unsub took a chance striking here. Especially so close to this road."

"He's either very bold or very desperate," Mia said, her comment catching the attention of an arriving police officer.

"Bold would my guess," the officer said. He was a forty-something man with broad shoulders, stocky frame and wisps of blonde hair that may as well not have been there. "Balls of steel if you ask me. I'm Martin Craven, the chief here."

The agents extended their hands. He had the firmest grip on the face of the earth, nearly pulling Ella's shoulder out of its socket. A good handshake always set the tone, Ella thought.

"I'm Agent Ripley and this is Agent Dark," Mia said. "Sorry for the delay in getting here. Busy morning."

"No apologies necessary. The body's been removed but the scene is still warm. As far as we can tell, we were on the scene within the hour so minimal contamination."

"Can you talk us through it?" Ella asked. She pulled out her notepad but it was mostly for effect. She tended to remember everything anyway. The chief led them across the yellow tape towards the death site.

"We got the call about 2am this morning. The victim's wife had called the hospital when her husband didn't come home. One of the

30

staff members checked out here and found his body in the bushes. James Floyd. One of the doctors here. We got here straight away."

"How was the scene when you found it?" Mia asked.

"Pretty clean, considering. The victim's car was locked, and the blood was confined to the small area by the bushes about fifty yards away."

"The entire attack took place in the bushes. The unsub must have lured the victim there."

"The un-what?" Craven asked.

"Unsub. It means unknown subject. FBI shorthand," Ella said.

"Gotcha," said Craven.

"Why was the victim here so late?" Mia asked.

"Night shift," Craven said. "He finished just after midnight. We estimate the time of death around half past midnight judging by the condition of the body, but we'll have an autopsy report within the next few hours."

They reached the murder location. The bushes where the attack had taken place had been parted to give officers a clearer view of the ground. Ella leaned down and inspected the soil. Patches of dried blood, some of which had flecked onto the concrete. She looked up and saw an entrance about fifty yards away.

"He took a real chance here," Ella said. "There could have been people coming and going through those doors over there."

"I'm surprised no one heard the screams. It doesn't look like this guy died quickly."

"That path is just for ambulances," Craven said. "I thought the same."

Ella turned to the sole vehicle in the parking lot. "That's the victim's car?"

"Yup. We've dusted it for prints and we're waiting on the results. We're hoping that if the altercation began at the car, the perp might have laid his hands on it."

"Mind if I check it out?" Ella asked.

"Go ahead."

Ella pulled out some gloves from her bag and made her way to the black sedan. Nothing looked out of the ordinary. It was immaculately clean both inside and out. No signs of damage anywhere. She got down on the floor and checked the tires. If the killer had purposely targeted James Floyd for whatever reason, there was a chance he might have impaired his vehicle in some way.

31

No slashed tires. Nothing lodged in the exhaust. Everything pointed to this being a random attack.

But as she inspected the concrete beneath the car, she spotted something.

She reached underneath, clawing for what looked like a table leg. Ella caught it between her fingertips and pulled it from underneath. She caught Mia's eye across the lot.

"What's that?" Mia called.

"No idea," Ella said. It was a rectangular piece of wood. Ella felt along and found one edge was sticky, like glue had been plastered across. She took it back to Mia and Craven. "This was underneath the victim's car. Seems a pretty strange place to leave a piece of wood."

"Get it to forensics," Mia said. "Our killer might have tried to hinder the victim's escape by sabotaging his car."

Mia passed it to Craven who took the object away. "This is a weird crime scene, Ripley," Ella said. "I can't make heads or tails of this thing. It seems really disjointed, like we're missing something that connects it all."

"Same. Why was our victim up in here in these bushes? Why did no one hear the attack? And why would our killer risk carrying out this crime outside a building full of people. This doesn't make for an easy profile, I'll be honest."

Ella agreed. There were no more answers to be found here, she thought. They needed to try another avenue.

"What if we went and inspected the bodies at the morgue? Maybe we'll find something the coroners have overlooked?"

Mia pocketed her notebook, then pulled out a pair of sunglasses. She adjusted her hair and put them on. Like everyone who applies sunglasses for the first time, she tested them by looking directly at the sun. A strange quirk of human psychology, Ella thought.

"You never struck me as a sunglasses person," she said.

"I'm not. I'm just not a sun person, either. Come on, let's pay a visit to the coroner's office. You're driving."

***

Ella mounted the curb outside the Mercer County Medical Examiner's Office on Livingston Avenue, much to the dismay of the line of traffic behind her.

"Just park it here," Mia said. She wasn't usually much of a backseat navigator, but she'd been a thorn in Ella's side the whole journey. Ella assumed the beaming sun had spiked Mia's irritation levels. Although in fairness to her, the humidity was quite distracting.

The agents stepped out of the car and entered a large foyer. Eerily quiet. Their footsteps reverberated around the room like measured gun shots until they approached the empty reception desk. A few seconds later, a young blonde lady rushed out.

"Can I help you?" she asked

Mia flashed her badge. "We've got an appointment with a Doctor Morris at 1pm."

The receptionist tapped away on her computer. "He's ready for you. Room 7B on your right." She passed them both lanyards and pointed in the direction behind her desk. The agents made their way down the hallway and found the room in question. Mia gave three hearty knocks.

A masked doctor opened it immediately. Even behind his protective equipment, Ella could sense the man's beaming smile. She'd met a lot of coroners during her time in the field, and they always seemed to be the happiest people around. Maybe dealing with death on a daily basis had some kind of life-affirming qualities to it.

"Come inside," the man said, holding the door wide. "I'm Doctor Morris. You must be the agents Craven told me about."

"Agent Dark and Agent Ripley," Ella said. "Thanks for seeing us so quickly."

The coroner took of his mask and hairnet and shook a mane of long brown hair loose. He had a chiseled face and eyes so green they could start traffic. Under other circumstances, she'd have felt that pang of attraction, but Mark had all but depleted her resources in the department. The mere thought of romance made her short of breath.

"My pleasure. Where do you ladies want to start?"

"James Floyd. Have you finished your tests on the body?" Mia asked.

"I literally sutured him up minutes ago. Here." He moved to one of the cabinets against the far wall, unlocked it and rolled out the doctor's body. "Strange circumstances, especially for a homicide victim."

James Floyd's body had taken on a yellow color. His skin had shrunk against the bone and his eyeballs had sunk, giving off the recently-deceased skeletal appearance. Ella had seen it plenty in the past, but it still hit her where it hurt every time. She recoiled not at the physical sight, but at what it represented: unnecessary loss. This poor man had a family; he helped people for a living. And here he was on a slab, gone before his time.

"What did you find?" asked Mia.

Doctor Morris picked up a long pointer and pointed to the victim's stomach. "One laceration through the abdomen, which perforated the victim's small intestine. This alone was enough to kill the victim, and most likely rendered him unable to move. Your attacker had this person at his mercy from this alone."

"But he killed him through strangulation?" offered Ella.

"Give that woman a cigar," Doctor Morris said. "The actual cause of death was asphyxiation, caused by compression of the neck and failure of the diaphragm and intercostal muscles. Now, here's where things get a little strange. Judging by the inflation of this man's lungs, he wasn't just strangled once. He was strangled again and again."

Ella wasn't sure she heard it right, or how it even made sense. "Huh? How?"

"When the body can't intake fresh oxygen, the lungs inflate to hold as much residual oxygen as they can. We consistently find it in people who've died by drowning or hanging. The lungs are around a centimeter more expanded than usual. But Mr. James Floyd here, his lungs were bloated twice the amount."

"How is that possible?" Mia asked. "I've never heard of that in my history of law enforcement."

"Because it's rare. I've read about it in medical textbooks but this is the first time I've seen it in person. I actually had to call my old teacher when I found it to double-check with him. Apparently it was common in Nazi concentration camps. When the Allies found the dead torture victims that hadn't been cremated, the ones who'd been drowned had bloated, abnormal-sized lungs, because they'd been pushed to the limit, brought up for air, then drowned again."

This was a lot to take in. Ella still wasn't sure what it meant. "Doctor Morris, do you mean this killer strangled the victim, then resuscitated him, then strangled him again?"

"Yes, that's exactly what he did. Each time, the lungs grew larger because they were prepared for the oncoming attack. Combined with the paralysis from his stomach wound, this man died in extreme, unimaginable agony."

Ella took off her glasses and took a step back. She needed a moment to process the new information. She could have done without Morris's descriptive language too.

"Jesus Christ," Mia said.

"Sorry," said Morris. "I hate to be the bearer of bad news. I hope I haven't upset you."

34

"We understand," said Mia. "Our killer really wanted this person to suffer. That's something we didn't expect. We profiled this as a random killing, but now that seems a tad too simple. How long would this process have taken, doctor?"

"Around four to five minutes by my estimate. It certainly wasn't quick. The medical tube that was present at the scene was simply theatre. It didn't impact James Floyd's death and was likely placed there post-mortem."

This cast the unsub in a whole new light. This was an act of sadism rather than convenience. This was a brutal inhuman slaying that called for a re-evaluation of the profile. "What about the first victim?" Ella asked.

Doctor Morris covered James's body with a sheet and then unlocked the next cabinet in line. He pulled out the corpse of victim number one.

"Leslie Buddington," Morris said. "On the surface, a simple killing, but actually quite complex once you dig past the surface."

Ella wasn't sure how to feel about this revelation. If this killer was actually more multifaceted than they expected, it meant they had a better chance of understanding his psychopathology. It was better in terms of understanding, but complex killers usually made fewer mistakes than their disorganized counterparts.

Doctor Morris moved his pointer to Leslie's groin area. "The femoral artery. The blood vessel that keeps your lower body functioning. You ladies are familiar with it?"

"Yes," Mia said.

Ella nodded. She'd heard of it, but that was as far as it went. No doubt Morris would educate her.

"Well, your attacker actually punctured Leslie's femoral artery with a single blow. That's not easy to do."

"Suggests medical knowledge?" asked Ella.

"Possibly. Either that or it was a lucky shot. Now, here's the thing. Much like James Floyd, this blow would have incapacitated Leslie. If he'd have simply left her, she'd have died within a minute."

Ella sensed a pattern. "But she didn't."

"But she didn't," Morris confirmed. "The amount of blood she passed was enough to kill her three times over, but somehow, Leslie stayed alive for several minutes."

By the look on Mia's face, even she was struggling to process the details. "How do you know that, doctor?" she asked.

Morris moved over to his computer screen and turned it around to show the agents. He navigated a picture folder and pulled one up. It showed a brown, scabby internal organ. Ella struggled to tell exactly which organ it was.

"This is her heart," Morris said. "It doesn't look like any heart you've seen before. You see these sores here? And these little black marks. That's from overwork and dehydration. Without blood to lubricate it, the heart and most other internal organs dry out very quickly."

"Hold up," said Mia. "I'm confused. So this killer bled the victim out, and somehow forced her heart to continue pumping, even though there was no blood to pump?"

"Pretty close," Morris said, moving back to Leslie's body.

"How the hell would he do that?" Mia asked. Ella was fighting back an overwhelming feeling of sickness.

"I found something quite strange inside her. A, uh…," Morris searched for the right word. "Cocktail."

"Drugs?" asked Ella.

"Medicines. Morphine, epinephrine, concentrated levels of salt and sugar. "

Ella tried to arrange the pieces together but couldn't quite form an accurate picture. Why would a healthy, 29-year-old woman have morphine in her system?

Mia put her hands on her hips and glanced between the body and the heart photograph. "Did you find any needle marks anywhere?"

Doctor Morris ran his pointer across Leslie's ribcage, then aimed it at the heart on the computer screen. Ella leaned closer and saw a tiny mark across the left breast.

"He did the same again," Ella said in disbelief. "He bled her out, then resuscitated her. He shot adrenaline into her heart."

"It certainly looks that way. He delivered the killing blow by strangulation. You can still see the marks around her neck where he wrapped the medical tube."

Ella had already spotted it on both victims. A white circle around the throats, like a translucent necklace.

"Ripley, this is unbelievable. He toyed with these victims like playthings. The opposite of everything we thought."

Mia wore an expression of bewilderment. It was clear she was as lost with this unsub as Ella was. "You're right. This is pure sadism, and there's still a lot I don't quite understand." Mia put her belongings back in her jacket. "Doctor Morris, thank you for your help. Could you send all the photographs over to Martin Craven at the NJPD please?"

"The chief. Will do," said Morris. "If I come across anything else, I'll let you know right away."

Ella couldn't quite get the image out of her head. These poor victims being kept on the edge of death just to satisfy some maniac's homicidal urges. Leslie and James should still be living their lives, providing care for the needy, but now they were locked in a cabinet until cremation rid their remains from this world.

Mia's phone pinged. She read the screen. "Come on Dark, we've been granted permission to visit James's wife. Let's go."

Ella gave her thanks to the doctor and walked out into the hallway. The lemon-scented odor was a welcome change from medical fluid and putrefaction, but Ella knew those sights wouldn't be leaving her mind's eye anytime soon.

Tobias Campbell suddenly felt like a million miles away. Her only thought was to hunt down the psychopath responsible for these cruel acts of barbarism.

CHAPTER SEVEN

Thirty minutes later, Ella and Mia pulled up outside James Floyd's house in the Rosedale area of Princeton. Ella thought it must have been the most expensive suburb she'd ever set foot in. Just looking at the cobblestone bungalows and lakeside farmhouses, she already felt like an outsider. This was a place for the elite.

"I bet you get some real types around here," Mia said.

"Agreed. I'd say we're amongst the upper echelons of society."

"Here," Mia said, pointing at house number 406. A wooden gate gave way to a vast lawn that covered more ground than her entire apartment complex. The grass had been patterned, like a football field.

She drove up and parked outside the door to the three-story home, her attention landing on the top-floor balcony that stretched across the width of the house. She saw deck chairs and a giant outside television. How the other half live, she thought.

A glass screen blocked off the entrance to the porch. The agents got out of the car, rang the bell and waited. A few seconds later, the doors slid open automatically. "Come in," a woman called.

Ella and Mia followed the path through. Ella was reluctant to lay her hands on anything, even the doorknobs, for fear of upsetting the faultless harmony on display. They entered into a lounge and found a middle-aged brunette sitting beneath a blanket on a white leather couch. Black eyeliner ran down her cheeks.

"Mrs. Floyd?" Mia asked.

"Julie, please. Take a seat," she said. Julie removed her blanket and piled it beside her. She sat upright, narrowly avoiding the empty wine bottles at her feet. She rubbed away her tears and smeared more makeup in the process.

The agents sat across the room on a long sofa. Ella admired the immaculate front room while Mia took the reins. There was a lengthy fish pond, nothing short of an aquarium, running along one of the walls. Beside them, some of James's awards hung on the wall. Winner of the New Jersey Top Doctor Recognition Program 2019, one of them declared.

"Please accept our sympathies. We're sorry we have to meet under such circumstances."

"I get it. Please just make it quick."

"Your husband seems like a very accomplished individual," Ella said.

"He was," Julie snapped, "and that's not making it quick. What do you want to know?"

She had intended to calm Julie down. It hadn't worked. Ella had learned by now that interviews with the bereaved never followed a format.

"Apologies. Could you tell us about James? How was he as a husband? What was your relationship like?"

"Fine. We've been married 22 years this month. Never had a hiccup in all that time."

Ella didn't quite believe it, but if there were any kinks in the relationship, they'd eventually come out. They always did.

"How about his work life?" Mia asked.

"James worked a lot," Julie shrugged. "He's always been very dedicated. But he's a doctor, what do you expect? He couldn't just clock off at 5 o' clock like everyone else."

"Of course. Was it ever a problem?" asked Mia.

"No. Never. I don't care how long he has to spend at the office. It's not like we didn't get enough time together."

Ella adjusted her position on the sofa. These things looked like a million bucks but they were a nightmare on the spine. She decided to get the tough questions out the way. It didn't feel like Julie was going to warm up to them anytime soon.

"Did James have any enemies at all? Maybe a co-worker? Or a patient he'd recently upset?"

Julie fingered the blanket beside her. She reached down and picked up a bottle of wine, shook it and then dropped it when she realized it was empty. "He had problems, yeah. But don't all people in that kind of job?"

"Problems how?" asked Mia.

"I don't know the specifics," Julie said. "He didn't really go into details. He'd just come home complaining that someone went off at him. Usually when he had to deliver bad news. He said he got used to it over the years, but I don't think he did. He was just keeping up appearances for me." Julie covered her face with her forearm, keeping fresh tears at bay.

"What about fellow employees? Anyone James didn't get along with?" asked Ella.

"No. They loved him. He was one of the few doctors at that hospital who gave a shit."

"How do you mean?" Mia said.

"James took his time with his patients. He connected with them. Even after they left his care, he'd call them up and see how they were doing. No doctor ever did that for me."

Ella felt a sudden new respect for their second victim. She'd never known a doctor do that before either.

"But I don't know what else you want me to tell you," Julie continued. "James was a saint. He'd never had any serious issues. He once got sued by the family of a patient but it fell through."

"Do you remember why he got sued?" asked Mia.

"Negligence or something. Something to do with end-of-life care. It was years ago though."

Ella made a note to check it out. Someone could still hold a grudge years on. Especially someone as sadistic as their unsub.

"Okay, we'll take a look," Mia said. "We're sorry we had to intrude on you like this, but your information could help us catch whoever did this."

"How? How could this help?" Julie said. She lay down on the sofa and reached for the remote control. She turned up the volume on the TV. Some daytime quiz show. Ella saw it regularly in the bereaved: distract yourself with trash media until the pain died down. It was a cheap fix but one that got results. She'd done it herself a few times.

"Sometimes it's the little things," Ella said. "Something as tenuous as a minor incident from decades before has helped catch serial killers in the past."

As soon as the term left her mouth, she knew she'd made a mistake of her own.

"Serial killer? You mean there are others as well as James?" Julie asked in shock.

Ella turned to Mia and expected to see that familiar face of disappointment. It wasn't there. Mia looked unconcerned.

"There are," Mia said. "One more. A woman from a local care home. Killed in the same manner as James."

Julie shot up like an uncoiled spring. "Who? What care home?" She seemed more concerned with this new information than the fact her husband had been murdered that morning.

"We can't release that information to the public," Mia said.

"Public? I'm not the public. I'm a victim as much as anyone else here."

"Still, we'd be jeopardizing the investigation if we…"

"Was it Tower Lodge Care Home?"

Both agents fell quiet for a second. They exchanged a glance. How would Julie know this? Lucky guess?

"What makes you think it was Tower Lodge?" Ella asked.

Julie fled into another room, leaving the agents alone. She returned seconds later with a framed photograph and threw it into Ella's lap. It showed eight people, standing poolside in front of a country vacation home.

Ella nearly dropped the photo when she saw two familiar faces.

"Oh God, Ripley, look."

Mia had already spotted it. James Floyd stood front and center, and Leslie Buddington stood to his right.

"Julie, where was this picture taken?" Mia asked.

"A few months ago, James was invited to a retreat with the workers from Tower Lodge. Some kind of seminar. I don't know what about exactly. And when James got back from there, he was… different."

"Different?" asked Ella.

"Like he didn't want to go into work anymore. He used to love going in, working hard, saving lives. After that retreat, it's like he lost his passion."

Ella scanned the other faces in the photograph. Aside from James and Leslie, there were four other women and two men, beaming smiles all around.

"How come you didn't mention this earlier?" Mia asked.

Julie rubbed her forehead. "I never really thought about it at the time. James was close to retirement anyway, but then you mentioned the retirement home and it all came back."

"Julie, could we keep this photo?" Ella asked.

"Okay. The other victim is one of them, isn't it?"

No more secrets, that's what Ella had told herself. It didn't matter whether it was to Mia or anyone else. "Yes it is," she said. "This blonde girl to James's right."

Julie curled back up on her sofa and directed her attention to the television. "Okay. Please leave me alone now. Do your job and catch this person."

"We will," Mia said, "thanks for everything." They took their leave and jumped back in the vehicle. Ella couldn't stop staring at the photo, for any of them could be the next victim or their killer.

***

Ella programmed the GPS back to Princeton Hospital. Now that it was late afternoon, they'd have a chance to speak to some of the staff who worked until the later hours with James. Mia took a phone call beside her but didn't say a whole lot. However, Ella could hear Edis's booming voice on the other end of the line.

She used the journey to collect her thoughts but wasn't quite sure where to start. The first and most important thing to address was that they'd profiled this killer completely wrong. These weren't in-and-out killings and judging by the new photograph, they might not have been victims of opportunity either. James and Leslie could very well have been purposely targeted, but for what reason? Why would someone have a vendetta against two people who dedicated their lives to helping others?

Then there was the bizarre killing method. Subdue, kill, revive, repeat. It was a very specific M.O. and one only used by one historical serial killer that she could recall. Serial killer Rodney Alcala would strangle his young, female victims to the brink of death and then resuscitate them, only to strangle them further. As far as she knew, no other murderer had ever incorporated this form of torture into their methodology before. And injecting chemicals into someone to keep them alive was completely unheard of by historical serial killer standards. Just when she thought she'd seen everything, someone came along and pushed things even further.

Worse still, her unsub had committed these acts in public. Usually, sadistic torturers sought out private places so they could take as long as they needed and savor the cruelty.

Now this photograph. Two victims in the same location. There was a chance it could be a coincidence, but the one rule that'd been drilled into her head was that detectives weren't allowed to believe in coincidences.

Mia ended her call with a defeated "okay, thank you" and turned to Ella. She reached into the back seat and pulled out the photo Julie had given them. "This is weird. What do you think?"

Ella was more interested in her conversation with Edis but she didn't want to push things. She'd ask when it felt right.

"Coincidence? Targeted attack? I don't know what to think right now."

"I want to focus on the link between the two victims for the time being. And we need to work out who these people in this photograph are, because they could be next."

"Or one of them could be our unsub."

"Maybe, but none of them seem to fit the physical profile. I still think this unsub is a smaller, weaker male, and the men in these photos look fairly built. But you're right, we still need to be sure."

Ella decided to muddy the waters. She wasn't convinced it was as straightforward as Mia made out.

"But if our unsub had the ability to resuscitate Leslie Buddington with a needle into the heart, wouldn't that suggest he had decent strength? Penetrating the ribcage isn't easy. Plus we know now that the initial stabbings weren't just to gain control, they were to prolong the victim's survival but keep them incapacitated."

Mia put her sunglasses back on and inspected the photo again. "Good point, Dark. That's why I keep you around. You could be onto something there."

Ella accepted the praise. After upsetting the last interviewee, she was feeling a little hollow. But she had to remind herself that this job was a constant stream of ups and downs. The only way to process things was to take the highs with the lows. "Thanks. Once we've been to the hospital, we'll head to the care home and identify these people."

Mia furiously typed something into her phone. Ella used the opportunity to take the conversation in another direction.

"Did the director have any news?" she asked.

Mia took a moment to respond. The silence hung in the air like a guillotine blade about to drop. "Nothing yet. No sightings of Tobias. No intel on his whereabouts. He's disappeared into the shadows. Edis has assigned some other agents to the case now."

"How is that possible?" Ella asked. "Wouldn't CCTV pick up the direction he went? Surely the hospital had cameras on the outside?"

"It did. They caught him walking out of the front and getting into a black SUV. No license plate. So he could be anywhere."

Ella imagined the scene. She didn't actually know how Tobias had escaped because Mia hadn't divulged the details. "Ripley, can you tell me how he got out? I need to know in case it was something to do with me."

"Something to do with you?"

Princeton Hospital came into view down the hill. Ella drove around the traffic and veered into the parking lot.

"You know what I mean. Like, what if I said something to him that helped him escape? Or if he foreshadowed it to me somehow. You know how he likes to play games."

"He faked an illness. Slowed his pulse down. Don't ask me how."

43

Ella knew exactly how. She knew because Tobias had mentioned it to her once, and she felt she had an obligation to tell her partner.

"It's a magic trick," she said.

"Magic?"

"Yeah. An illusion. Or *pattern recognition exploitation* as he called it."

Mia didn't respond. She just looked out of the window. Ella felt like she'd crossed a boundary, but surely it was better to be one hundred percent transparent with her partner.

"How?" Mia finally asked.

"You put something in your armpit and it stops the blood flow to the radial pulse. It makes you look like you're dying."

"God damn it," Mia said. "They found a tiny ball at the crime scene. They had no idea where it came from or why it was there."

"Crime scene?" Ella asked. "What do you mean?"

Mia hesitated slightly as Ella parked their car outside the hospital doors. She killed the engine and turned to her partner who was shunning eye contact. "Ripley? What crime scene?"

Mia took off her sunglasses and rubbed her face. "Look, I didn't want to tell you this, Dark, because I know how you'll take it."

Ella clutched her keys so hard they cut into her skin. "Tell me what? Please, I need to know. This involved me as much as anyone else."

"You take things personally, rookie. I need your attention on this case, not on Tobias, alright?"

Ella refused. She had a right to know the goings-on. If blood was on her hands, she'd accept it, as painful as it would be.

"Ripley, I'm not leaving this car until you tell me. Did Tobias kill someone?"

Mia checked her phone again, stalling by the looks of things. "Three people. He killed three people."

Ella pushed open the car door and stuck her head out. She needed air, or she was going to vomit. She pushed her forearm into her stomach to keep the bile down.

"Three people? Are you kidding me? How? Who were they?"

"Guards from Maine State. And a nurse," Mia said.

Ella shot out of the car, stood up and leaned against it. These three victims, they died because of her. It was she who rattled the cage and released the beast inside, and so she was responsible for everything that followed. Her head began to spin in circles and she was sure that any moment now, this morning's coffee would hit the pavement.

"I told you, Dark. It's not your fault. You can't take responsibility for the actions of a psycho." Mia slammed her door shut and joined her. "You visited him. That was all. You didn't unlock his cell. Tobias must have been planning this for a long time. It has nothing to do with you."

"We don't know that," Ella shouted. "It could have absolutely been because of me. He obviously wants to kill me, and that motivated him to escape. I'm the catalyst to all this."

Ella wanted to get in the car, drive right through to Maine and tear through every inch of that state until she found him.

But she couldn't. Not yet, at least.

"We'll deal with this later," Mia said. "Come on, I need you to focus. If your mind is somewhere else, we'll never be able to catch this killer. Now, are you with me or not?"

Ella composed herself. A few passers-by eyed the agents with suspicion. She ignored them.

Mia was right. Finding one killer was hard enough, finding two was impossible. "I'm with you. One killer at a time."

CHAPTER EIGHT

He sat on a bench beside a river, looking up at the high-rise building in the distance. Today was the first time in 16 years he'd smelled fresh morning air, and it was just as sickening as it was back then. But even so, he liked it here. Nobody had passed him by in hours, only wandering horses from the farm down the way. That was fine by him. He'd give it a few more hours here, then find somewhere to hide out once dusk fell.

This was a different world than what he remembered. Although his experience had been limited so far, today's people seemed a lot more compliant, less intrusive. That old rebellious spirit that was so common in his day seemed to be non-existent. He'd walked through busy streets with a hood up and not a single person had given him a second glance. Whatever was on their cell phones must have been incredibly important, since barely anyone looked up from them. Even the security guard, when he'd walked out of the store with pockets full of food, was glued to his phone screen.

But that just made his task a little easier. He had everything he needed so far. A place to hide. A place to sleep. Enough sustenance to keep him going. He had friends in the right places, even ones that could ferry him from Maine to Washington in a matter of hours. They'd transported him in the back of a van like some vital military cargo, dropped him off and gave him the location of the safe spots around the city. So far, he hadn't needed them, but he might have to call upon them when night fell.

How long would it be before the authorities came crashing down on him? What measures had the FBI set up to get him back behind bars? His intel hadn't come through yet since he had no way of receiving it. He'd been offered a cell phone by one of his contacts, but turned it down out of forethought. If he had a signal, that meant they could track him. He knew that if they caught him again, it would be an expedited trip to the gallows. They weren't going to risk locking him up. Straight to the grave, secrets and all.

And that could very well happen. He wasn't naïve enough to believe he could evade detection for the rest of his life. Even with all his disciples and his underground associates, someone, somewhere would recognize him. Then eager cops would be on him like a fly to feces, taking him back to the glass cell or putting a bullet in his head right there. He had no desire to live in solitude for the rest of his days because it would be no different than being in prison. He was going to live his life, do the things he'd always planned on, and most importantly, make amends for everything that went wrong.

First and foremost, was the lady in his life. The thorn in his side. The woman who'd provoked him into finally putting his escape plan into action and getting back into the outside world. It had been a long time in development, but the thought of twisting the head off her neck drove him to new heights of determination.

Only a few hours ago, he'd seen her in the flesh for the third time. Now that he was outside of the confines of his prison cell, things felt a little different. Like two old friends who'd miraculously bumped into each other a long way from home. This time, there was nothing stopping him reaching out and touching her, feeling his skin on hers, and the idea sent stimulating waves through his whole body. In this new setting, he almost felt a connection with her. He had seen her in her natural habitat, going about her day, mingling with what he assumed was her boyfriend. While he could sense that hers and his existence were probably comparable, he would feel nothing when he prematurely ended her life. It was a necessity, a part of the game he had planned.

But that wasn't the person he wanted. Miss Dark was just a sacrificial pawn in his game. And if ripping her limbs off added to his real target's torment, then that was a necessary step in the process.

Miss Dark would die, and she would learn the true depths of which the psychopathic mind was capable, just like she wanted. Hadn't she originally come to him to learn exactly that?

Yes, she would die as planned, but the real target here, and always had been, was Agent Mia Ripley.

CHAPTER NINE

Ella and Mia split up around the hospital to cover more ground. Ella had spoken to about fifteen people within the hour, and none of them had a bad word to say about James Floyd. He seemed to be universally loved throughout Princeton Hospital, even more so with the long-term patients under his care.

She sat in James Floyd's office, now unoccupied out of respect for his recent passing. His desk was a mass of paperwork and stationery, reminding Ella of the pile of documents she left on her lounge floor back at home. She idly flipped through them. A photograph of James and Julie sat next to his keyboard. Ella quickly rummaged through his drawers, finding overspill from his desk. More documents, endless pens, a worn out stamp. She scanned a document of a recently deceased patient named Marcus Heroux then pushed it aside, not wanting to consume the details of the dead.

Then she found something silvery.

Ella moved some files out of the way and picked up the unexpected item. It was a silver chain, old and faded, but still pretty sturdy. A necklace.

A knock on the door startled her. She dropped the piece of jewelry on the desk and quickly shut the drawers. "Hello?" she called, as if the office was her own.

"Sorry," a voice said before they'd even entered the room. A woman walked in, late fifties by Ella's guess, dressed in blue scrubs. She had short brown hair and giant glasses that magnified her eyes to uncanny levels. "I didn't mean to bother you. I thought this office was empty."

"My fault," Ella said. "I'm with the FBI, just looking into Doctor Floyd's life."

"Oh, well I won't interrupt. I just came to see if he had any spare syringes in here. We're running low out on the floor."

Ella waved her to continue. "Carry on. Don't mind me."

"FBI, eh? Thank God. We're all scared to go outside after what happened to Doctor Floyd."

"Did you know him?" Ella asked.

"Everyone knew James. A real doctor's doctor. Old fashioned gent who gave things a personal touch. Hard to come by nowadays." The nurse began to search through the doctor's cupboards along the wall.

"Could you tell me anything about him? Anything that might help us out here. By all accounts, James was a saint."

"Oh, he was. I worked with him for... God, must be fifteen years now. You won't find a soul around here who didn't like him."

Ella watched the woman work, and her antique image and short locks reminded her of one of Harold Shipman's victims. Shipman had been one of the most prolific serial killers of all time, racking up an estimated 120 deaths over a 20 year career. He'd been a local doctor who injected old women with morphine, recreating the scene of his own mother's death over and over again. His face had been on her mind ever since she found out the medical connection of this case, but Shipman was a doctor killing patients, not the other way around.

"Got them," the nurse continued. She cupped around ten boxes in her arms. "Oh, you found James's lucky charm," she laughed.

Ella followed the woman's stare. It was pointed at the necklace on the desk between them. "Oh, this? I just found it among his stuff. I'm guessing it was his jewelry."

"No, no, that wasn't James's. That was Neville's. He gave it to him."

The nurse had clearly missed a few steps in the story. "Neville? Another worker here?"

"No. Neville was a patient. Long-term patient, was in here for about six months by my count. Old guy, terminal. James was real good to him, treated him like his own dad. James was a sucker for that."

"Oh, I've heard that James got pretty close to his patients. I respect him for that," Ella said.

"Yeah, well, there was a real hoo-ha around the whole thing. We had a nurse here that really screwed up Neville's medication. Ended up killing him early. He and James got into a whole spat. That necklace turned into James's lucky charm after that."

The nurse suddenly had Ella's attention. "Hold up, James got into a fight with another worker?"

"Oh yeah, he got the kid fired."

"What?" Ella said. "Why has no one told me about this?" She suddenly remembered the Shipman case again. The true extent of his crimes didn't come out for years, and by then he'd already moved through multiple practices around the country.

49

Of course, she realized, hammering her fist on the table. This unsub didn't have to be in the hospital *now,* but could have left a long time ago.

"Not many people knew, to be honest. James kept it hush-hush. He felt bad for the kid, but them's the brakes."

"Do you have this nurse's name?" Ella asked. "Or can you describe him?"

"God, now you're asking." One of the boxes fell out of her grip. She adjusted and picked it up. "Young kid, fresh off the block. Real black eyes, like them children of the corn. You're shit out of luck if I'm remembering his name though. I got three grandkids and I still get them mixed up."

Ella shot up out the chair with renewed passion. "Is there anyone around here who might?" she asked.

"There just might be. Here, follow me sweetheart."

***

The plaque on the door said *HUMAN RESOURCES OFFICE.* Through the circular glass window, Ella saw a lone woman sitting behind a desk. The woman caught her eye and smiled, which Ella saw as an invitation to enter.

"Hi, Miss…"

"Adams. Kelly Adams. Can I help you?" she asked. She was about forty years old with short blonde hair and some nicotine-stained teeth.

Ella shut the door behind her. "Miss Adams, my name's Agent Dark and I'm with the FBI. We're currently looking into the death of a recent employee here."

"Doctor Floyd. I'm knee-deep in that myself. A guy gets killed and the only thing the bosses care about is paperwork. That's bureaucracy for you."

Ella had never a met HR rep she liked, but Kelly Adams might be the first. "Don't I know it?" Ella said. "I was wondering if I could pick your brain about something. Something to do with James's past."

"I can try," Kelly said. She pushed her mouse out of range, looking more than eager to do something other than administration. "What is it you need to know?"

"A nurse here just told me that James had a run-in with another co-worker. I'm not sure when exactly. She mentioned negligence, and that this co-worker ended up fired because of James. Is that something you recall?"

"I recall it very well. The only problem is I'm not sure if I'm allowed to talk about it."

"Please, Miss Adams, this could be exactly what we need. If this co-worker held a grudge, it's not impossible for him to stretch to murder."

Kelly locked eyes with Ella for a moment. She pored over Ella's comment.

"Alright. If it helps catch whoever did this, I'm in, but keep it off the record. If anyone asks, you got this from someone else here, not me."

Ella nodded. She loved off the record. Kelly dug into her drawers and pulled out a folder. She quickly scanned the contents.

"It all happened about a year ago. There was a nurse here named Connor Jansen. He was one of the trainees under Doctor Floyd. They had a terminal patient under their care, and Floyd put his life expectancy at around one year. The patient died after six months and the family demanded an inquiry. It came out that he'd been administered much higher doses of morphine than recommended."

Ella's spine tingled when she heard the word morphine. She felt like another piece of the puzzle had fallen into place. There was something here, she knew it.

"Was Doctor Floyd suspected of anything?" Ella asked.

"No. The culprit was very clear. We had documentation and CCTV footage backing it up. Connor Jansen had dispensed the excessive dosages. Exactly why, we don't know. He claimed it was an accident."

She thought of the Shipman case again, along with endless other *angel of death* killers. Michael Swango, Donald Harvey, Kristen Gilbert. They were a very rare type of killer; medical officials who murdered those they were meant to care for. Even though their unsub wasn't an angel of death, it didn't mean he didn't start out as one.

"And this caused a rift between James Floyd and Connor Jansen?"

"You could say that. It went to court. Private case, not many knew about it, but I could tell it tore James up a little. I'm not sure of the outcome though."

That was fine, Ella could find that information herself in seconds. She quickly ran through the events in her head from start to finish and everything connected. If this Connor person had a sadistic mind, he may have murdered the terminal patient for kicks. It was no secret that the medical world attracted its fair share of psychopaths. In fact, in a list of professions with the highest number of psychopaths, medical experts came in third just after police officer and CEO.

"And where is this Connor Jansen now?" she asked.

"I couldn't tell you," Kelly said. "After we fired him, I never heard from him again."

Ella had to find Mia and quickly. This could be the break they needed. "Thank you, you've been a tremendous help," she said.

"No problem, but remember, this didn't come from me. I don't need the hassle of explaining myself to the top dogs."

"Your secret's safe with me," Ella said as she moved for the door. "One last thing before I leave you in peace. Was this Connor Jansen person particularly violent? Maybe something a little off about him?"

Kelly Adams filed away the document and grabbed her computer mouse again. Without looking away from her screen, she said, "yes, I think so."

"You do?"

"Off the record again, but yeah. The kid was a liability from day one. Lazy, shabby, a real creep. But that's just one woman's opinion."

"It's enough," Ella said.

Kelly passed across her business card. "Any questions, call my cell. Don't call anyone else."

Ella nodded her thanks, left the room and called the number the police chief had given her earlier. He answered after two rings.

"Hello?"

"Chief Craven, it's Agent Dark. Could you do something for me real quick?"

The chief adjusted something in the background. Ella heard a deafening crunch down the phone line.

"Sure, hit me as hard as you got."

"I need a search on a local guy named Connor Jansen." She spelled the name for him. "He worked at Princeton Hospital but got let go for negligence. A patient died under his care." She heard Craven typing away.

"You think it's related?" he asked.

"There's more. James Floyd had to testify against him in court. This Connor character could have been looking for vengeance."

"Alright, just searching now. Hold the line."

Ella kept the phone to her ear while she navigated the labyrinthine hospital walkways. Mia could be anywhere in this maze. Medical staff, patients, and families rolled past her. Down the phone line, she heard the chief chattering away to someone else.

Then he went quiet.

A little too quiet.

"Chief Craven? Are you still there?" she asked.

"Uh huh, I'm here, it's just…"

His voice trailed off again.

"Is everything okay?"

"Miss Dark, I'm going to send you something. I think you need to see this."

"What is it?" she asked. It sounded promising, despite Craven's ominous tone.

Ella heard her inbox ping. She turned the call to speakerphone and navigated to her email. Chief Craven had sent her a screenshot from Connor Jansen's trial documents.

She saw it immediately.

"Oh my God," she said. Her pace turned into a brisk walk, then to a breakneck run. She ended her call with the chief.

Mia needed to see this ASAP.

CHAPTER TEN

Mia had somehow found herself in the maternity ward, among big-bellied women wearing the whole spectrum of expressions. Anxiety, panic, delight. Maybe she'd subconsciously sought this department out because the ward was mostly associated with pleasant vibrations. Everywhere else featured hubs of death, illness, and bad news.

A passer-by handed her a leaflet. *SECOND HAND SMOKE CAUSES CANCER IN CHILDREN*. Okay, maybe it wasn't all pleasant here.

Mia found herself wishing that, for once, one of their victims would have a seriously dirty past. She'd questioned about 20 people about their relationships with James Floyd, and every single one of them had sung his praises to high heaven. As far as she could tell, he was an angel in a doctor's uniform, and not a single person could identify any reason why someone might want to hurt him.

Why couldn't he have been having an affair with a stripper? Why couldn't he owe money to the wrong people? Dirt created avenues to explore. It was the squeaky clean victims who slipped right through their grip. James Floyd was the latter, and if the answer to his demise lay in this hospital, Mia wasn't able to find it.

Pounding footsteps cut through the chorus of idle chatter, and all eyeballs in the corridor looked towards the source of the disturbance. A figure in boots and a brown jacket ran down the hallway, hair flowing behind her like a satin scarf. Even in such a blur, Mia recognized the figure.

"Dark," she called out. The rookie looked around, eventually catching Mia's eye. She looked like she'd just run a marathon.

"Ripley, here you are. Don't you check your phone?"

"No reception in here. What's wrong? Didn't anyone tell you it's rude to run down corridors?"

Ella ignored the comment. "Look, I found something. Something massive."

She knew she could count on the rookie to deliver the goods. "Well, I'm glad you did, because I feel like I've been banging my head against a wall. What have you got?" Mia scanned the room and saw all the big-bellied ladies and concerned partners staring holes through them. The last thing she wanted to do was give these poor folk any reason to panic. Their heart rates were high enough already. She ushered Ella away from the rabble.

"Tell me everything."

Ella caught her breath pretty quickly. How Mia envied the advantages of youth and physical fitness.

"I spoke to HR. They told me that James Floyd had to testify against a former co-worker at a trial recently."

This sounded good. Finally, a motive. "Oh yeah? What happened?"

"There was a male nurse named Connor Jansen. A *real creep* according to the HR woman."

"Sounds like my kind of HR woman. What did Jansen do?"

"He over-supplied a patient with morphine. Killed him. They launched an investigation into the death and found Jansen was the person responsible. James Floyd testified against him and put him behind bars."

"Dark," Mia said. "Think about that for a second."

"No, he's not in jail anymore. He got out... two weeks ago."

Now she had Mia's attention. "Great work, Dark. Looks like a pretty good suspect. Do you..."

"There's more," Ella interrupted. "Look at this. The chief just sent it over to me."

Mia could hardly believe how fast she'd worked. She was suddenly reminded of her ex-partner who spent most of their case looking confused and blowing up service stations. It was nice to have a competent buddy by her side again.

Ella stuck her phone screen in Mia's face. Mia adjusted her eyes to the tiny text but just saw a jumble of words and names.

"What am I looking at here?" Mia asked.

"This is a transcript from the trial. Look at who else testified against him."

Mia pushed the screen away to a readable distance. She saw the name immediately. "God damn. Leslie Buddington was there too."

"Yeah, she witnessed Jansen's negligence in person according to this. That's a link to both victims. We have to pay this guy a visit right this second."

This was the Ella Dark she liked to see. Not the anxiety-ridden girl who blamed herself for murders out of her control. Not the betrayer who kept deadly secrets to herself. The girl who made headway regardless of the barriers, and if she happened across a brick wall, she'd break it down with her fists. This was the kind of partner Mia needed and she wasn't going to let the rookie slip away again. She'd been a fool to do so the first time but she was happy to admit her mistake.

Before getting here, Mia noticed that the rookie wasn't herself. Something had rattled her, right from the moment they left Washington for New Jersey. The logical answer was relationship trouble with Mark. Two agents, always on the road, constant time away from each other. It wasn't a good foundation for a relationship, but Mia couldn't outright tell the rookie that. Some things you had to learn the hard way.

"Yes we do. Let's go. You got this guy's address?" They made their way out into the afternoon air towards the parking lot.

"The chief has already sent it across. He lives about six miles from here."

"Perfect proximity," Mia said. "He'll already be familiar with these areas if he's worked here, so he'd have known when best to strike."

"Exactly what I thought," Ella said. "I haven't seen his picture but I can already guess what he looks like. Weedy, skinny, nervous, introverted."

"I'm guessing the same. Come on, time to see him for ourselves."

***

Connor Jansen's address was a studio apartment tucked away behind a row of shops in downtown Princeton. Not exactly the most pleasant area in the city, but it must have cost a pretty penny. That raised Ella's suspicions even further.

She parked their car out of sight, stood on the sidewalk, and surveyed the area. She familiarized herself with the layout in case Connor took the coward's way out. And she'd met enough people like him to know that was usually how it played out.

Ella had a good feeling about this. Connor fit the mold down to a tee and that was good enough for her. Her only worry was that the suspect had anticipated their arrival and was either ready to attack or had already fled.

"Dark, I've got a feeling this guy is going to haul ass," Mia said.

"You read my mind. How should we play it?"

"You found this guy. You did the hard work. You take the lead. What do you want to do?"

A surge of new confidence overcame her. She appreciated the gesture. It was nice to be gifted authority once in a while. "Alright, I'll go up and knock on the door. There's only one way down, so you wait here for him. If he yields straight away, then just come up and join us."

"Sounds like a plan," Mia said. She positioned herself at the bottom of the staircase leading up to the row of apartments. Ella walked up and found number 4. From this vantage point, she could see a row of garages below and a few stores on the other side. She didn't think anyone would be stupid enough to jump right off this balcony, but if Connor tried anything of the sort, Mia would be there to catch him.

Ella knocked on the door and waited. It was 4pm and dusk was beginning to set in. Most people were just coming home from work, but according to Connor's record, he'd been unemployed since he left Princeton.

No one answered. Ella knocked again and pressed her ear to the door. Nothing. She pressed her to the spyglass and saw a blurry interior, but a blur that was in motion.

Someone was in there.

She hammered on the door and went for broke. "Connor Jansen. I'm with the FBI. Please open up immediately."

She suppressed the initial adrenaline rush, saving it for a more crucial time.

Then the door opened, slowly and hesitantly. A face peered around the door, and not the one Ella expected.

"Hello?" the voice said, soft spoken and fearful. "Who are you?"

"Are you Connor Jansen?" Ella asked. The man was suited and booted in a gray three-piece. He had short black hair combed over to one side and deep, bulging eyes like a deep-water fish. He was quite tall and seemed to be in impeccable shape. Not the wiry creature she'd expected.

"I might be. Why?"

"I'm Agent Dark with the FBI. I'd like to talk to you about an incident at Princeton Hospital last year."

"Is this about Floyd again?" Connor asked. "How many times do I have to talk to you people? I've already said everything I have to. I'm not talking about it anymore."

"Is it true you were involved in a case of patient neglect?" Ella asked, not letting the conversation end so abruptly. So far, he showed no signs of wanting to flee. He stood firm, both feet planted on his doormat.

"You already know I was, so why are you asking? I did my time and I hated every second of it. What else is there to talk about? I made a mistake and got punished for it. End of story."

Ella felt that familiar brick wall appearing in front of her. She had to break it down if she wanted answers. The answer, as always, was to push the suspect's buttons. Force their emotions to the forefront.

"Why did you do it, Mr. Jansen? Did you enjoy it? Was it a trial for something bigger?"

Connor grabbed the door as though he was about to slam it in Ella's face. He didn't, but she saw his expression turn bitter.

"What? Are you trying to piss me off?"

"No, I'm just asking questions."

A second voice shouted from inside the house. Connor turned away from Ella and shouted to the invisible resident. "It's nothing, just a friend," he called.

"Bad time?" Ella asked. "Why don't we talk more down at the precinct?"

"Yes it is a bad time, and I can't."

"Well, you might not have a choice," Ella said.

Connor glanced back into the darkness of his apartment and called out again. He turned back to Ella. "Look, can we talk inside?"

She was a little shocked. She hadn't expected an invitation. "Sure. Let's do that." She gave Mia a thumbs-up, but then waved her hand in a dismissive gesture. She didn't need Mia for this. She was going to bring this guy down on her own.

Before opening the door, Connor leaned into her. Ella readied herself to strike, but Connor just whispered in her ear, "If she asks, tell her you're my friend. Please?"

"Uhm, okay," Ella said. "Who?"

Connor ignored her question, opened the door and walked down the dim hallway. At the end, they turned into a lounge decorated as though it belonged to a previous era. The shabby brown carpet squelched beneath her feet and there were noticeable stains on the single brown couch.

But when Ella saw the room's unintended focal point, her heart leaped into her throat.

"Oh my God," she said. Like a light switch, her attitude towards this gentleman did a 360-turn. Was he their unsub? Maybe, but it looked like he had a heart somewhere among the cruelty and homicidal rage, if it existed.

In one corner of the room, she saw an elderly woman lying on a small bed. She had tubes sprouting from her arm, one up her nose, and a heart rate monitor to her side.

"Mom, this is my friend," Connor said. "We're just going into the next room."

"Don't be late," the woman said, punctuating after every word. Connor escorted Ella into the kitchen area, out of earshot of his mother.

"Make this quick," Connor said. "What do you want to know?"

Ella got right to the point. Clearly the poor woman in the next room depended on Connor for her survival. "I want to know where you were at midnight last night and midnight on April 30."

"Why?" Connor asked, dropping his voice to a whisper.

Ella did the same, not wanting to give Connor's mother a reason to be paranoid. "Because we're investigating two murders, both of whom have connections to you."

Connor slipped against the messy kitchen top. He grabbed a cupboard to keep his balance. "What are you talking about? What murders?"

Ella couldn't tell if Connor was being truthful or putting on a show. She made sure to watch his micro signals closely. She wished she'd have invited Mia up now.

"The murders of Leslie Buddington and James Floyd. Two people I believe you're very familiar with."

Connor's pale face turned paler. He arched himself over the sink and ran the tap at full force. Connor coughed violently for a second, drank from the tap then spat the water out. If it was an act, it was a good one.

"You're familiar with these people, yes?" Ella asked.

Connor drank more water but swallowed it this time. He caught his breath. "Yes, of course. I worked with them."

"And they testified against you in court."

"Yes they did, but I don't hold any grudges against them. They caught me. I paid the price, but that chapter is over. They're both really dead? What happened?"

Ella didn't buy it, at least not fully. Or maybe she was clinging onto the misplaced hope that Connor Jansen could be their unsub. "You got out of prison a few weeks ago, is that correct?"

"Yes, and I'm starting again, but this little meeting is putting a stop to that."

"So, you can tell me where you were on those nights?" Ella said. A part of her hoped that Connor wasn't their man, because he seemed to be down on his luck. But at the very least, he'd killed a patient he was supposed to care for and she couldn't overlook that.

"Yes, I was at work. I'm part of a rehabilitation program. I work night shifts at Smyth's Haulage Depot. I've been there every night this week."

"And you can prove this?"

"Yeah. I got clock cards. People saw me. We have cameras too."

Ella unwound a little and rested against the kitchen door. She'd have to get someone to check the cameras, but she knew exactly what she'd find. A dead end. For all his compatibility with the profile, Connor Jansen wasn't her man. It was a bitter pill to swallow, but a part of her was relieved.

They both waited in silence for a moment. Ella wanted to make sure she'd covered all avenues before leaving. "Why did you do it?" she asked.

"I just told you, I didn't," Connor said.

"Not that. The patient at Princeton Hospital. Why did you overdose him?"

Connor peered his head around the door to check on his mom. She hadn't made a sound since they'd entered the kitchen.

"Practice," Connor said.

Ella wasn't sure she heard him right. "Practice? What for?"

"My mom. I'm all she's got. We can't afford healthcare so it was up to me. I wasn't sure how much medication to use on her so I... used a test subject. I confessed all this in court."

Ella hadn't had time to read through the whole court case yet. She cursed herself for not looking at the whole picture before acting.

"I'm sorry to hear that, but it was wrong to do."

"I know it's wrong. I knew it was wrong back then. But desperation makes you do stupid things."

Ella couldn't argue. Desperation had driven her to some foolish lows herself.

"When I got out of jail, I made a promise to better myself. I was actually on my way to a job interview before you got here. A real job, not some exploitation of cheap labor."

"Oh God, I'm so sorry. I'll let you get going."

"Too late now," Connor said. "Probably missed my bus."

Ella glanced into the lounge. It was a sorry sight. This poor woman, likely on the verge of death. A distressed son doing everything to keep her alive. She knew that if her dad was still around, she'd do everything she could do sustain him too.

Connor slipped his shoes off and sat on the kitchen counter. "Leslie and Doctor Floyd? I'm... sorry to hear that."

60

Ella jumped out of her chair. "Shoes on. Now. I'll take you where you need to be."

Connor dropped down to his feet. "What? Really?"

"Yes, let's go." She couldn't begrudge anyone for trying to better themselves, especially when it was motivated by selflessness. Connor dressed himself and led the way out. Ella turned to the boy's mother.

"I'm sorry to have interrupted, Mrs. Jansen. I wish you all the best."

The woman waved dismissively. She looked half-asleep.

"Will she be okay on her own?" Ella asked.

"She'll be fine. I'll only be an hour anyway."

The two exited the home and went down the staircase to where Mia was waiting. She had a beaming grin. Ella jumped in before Mia could say anything.

"Ripley, I've got some bad news."

CHAPTER ELEVEN

Contented and tingling from his kills, he sat near the window of Aunt Betty's Café and sipped his coffee. From here, he could watch the world go by and sense the mood of the city. He overheard conversations, all of them on the same subject. By now, news of his activities had reached the masses, and it seemed everyone he brushed past had an opinion to share. He commiserated with the waitress who mentioned them to him, but secretly reveled in her distress.

It was an addictive feeling, something he hadn't quite expected. In his mind, these were kills of necessity, ridding the world of those who'd wronged him. The weeks he'd spent summoning the courage now seemed like a world away, and if he'd have known it was this thrilling, he wouldn't have wasted time worrying.

Cursory glances came his way, and each one sparked a wave of anxiety. Did someone know his secret? Or were they just staring in pity at the lonely man in the coffee shop? Perhaps the locals were just on edge now, eyeing every new face with reverent suspicion?

No one could know he was the person responsible. He'd been careful, meticulous. Watched from the shadows and struck at the optimal time. He was as invisible as a predator could be.

A week ago, he would have kept his head down, averted his eyes whenever someone glanced his way. But now he eyed the room with a newfound dominance, imagining exactly what torment he could unleash upon these perfect strangers. One of the girls in here looked just like the nurse. Young, blonde, gentle blue eyes. Maybe he'd follow her home, learn her schedule and strike once the urge came back. Maybe killing someone random would throw the cops off the scent?

No, he had a mission and he had to stick to it. Besides, these people meant nothing to him. When he left those other mangled corpses in his wake, the thrill came from the fact he was making amends for what they'd done to him.

This was vengeance as high art. Killing them wouldn't bring her back, but it was the closest he'd get. He'd held her hand as she died and promised right there and then that justice would be done.

Two down, two to go.

And just as he downed his coffee, number three walked out of the store across the street.

He almost felt sorry for the frail old man. The last time he'd seen him, he'd been much healthier, much trimmer. Now he was struggling to walk by the looks of things.

He'd watched him enter the store, just like he did every Saturday evening for the past few months. He must have been a lonely old gent, doing his grocery shopping while most people were out. It would make for an easy kill, and this time, he'd get time to actually savor it.

The old gentleman put his bags on the floor, unlocked his silver Mercedes and slowly loaded them in. The man in the coffee shop got irritated just watching him. How slow did one man have to be? Get a move on, you old bastard. Didn't he know he had a big evening planned?

He exited the coffee shop, leaving a $5 tip. Recent events had improved his mood somewhat, and there was a new sense of charity among the contentment. In the tiny parking lot, he got in his car, slowly drove out and curbed it at the bottom of the street. In his rear-view mirror, he watched the silver Mercedes roll out into the street and drive right past him.

And he followed, keeping a discreet two-car distance apart. If the past was any indicator, the old man was going home now to watch trash television and drink wine until he passed out. A pretty pathetic existence. He doubted anyone would miss him.

They exited the town into the suburbs. He had to be careful, because if any CCTV picked up that he'd followed him for several miles, cops would descend on him. Luckily, he'd been planning this long enough to know every move by muscle memory. He drove through the twisty-turny residential streets, now having lost sight of the silver Mercedes.

But then he went past the old man's home, and sure enough, he was outside his front door, struggling with his groceries again.

He ignored him and carried on, trying not to imagine just how glorious it was going to be to choke the life from the old man in just a few hours.

Right on cue, the masses descended upon the tavern at the end of the old man's street. He parked his car along with the others, hidden among the crowd. He couldn't just leave it in the middle of the street because, knowing the residents in this area, someone would spot it. He got out of the car, walked inside the tavern and took a seat.

Waiting came next. He'd leave in two hours, three at most. He could easily distract himself, maybe even chat with a few regulars, get their opinion on the recent murders.

Then once that was done, he'd add number three to the list, and this one was going to be the best one yet.

CHAPTER TWELVE

It was early evening, but rather than head to their motel, Ella and Mia checked into their new office at the NJPD precinct. A wonderfully bare room, deep gray walls and no windows. It was everything Ella needed to figure things out.

She turned off her phone because the constant buzzing had started to drive her crazy. She hadn't noticed until now, but Mark had already bombarded her with text messages throughout the day and they showed no signs of slowing down. She really thought that chapter was over, but it seemed Mark's determination was as unkillable as Tobias Campbell's.

Nine messages, 2 missed calls, and a voicemail. When was this guy going to get the message, and what could she possibly do to make this stop? It was like arguing with a toddler. He didn't listen; he just heard what he wanted to.

Mia walked in, eyes glued to her phone. She threw it on the table and took a seat opposite her partner. Since the dead end with Connor Jansen, Ella had sensed a little tension between her and Mia. Mia had obviously been ecstatic that they could solve this one and start making headway on the Tobias case, but the setback had sent her into a spiral of exasperation.

"That was one of the other officers. Jansen's alibi checks out. We're back to square one."

Ella had already come to terms with it, but it didn't make it any easier to digest. This one hindrance amplified the other problems, and Ella wished she could just click her fingers and make everything right again.

But that wasn't an option. If she wanted things back to normal, hard work was the only solution.

"I guessed as much."

"Let's just keep searching, I suppose."

Ella watched her partner open up her laptop. Mia stared at the screen, and Ella saw that Mia's eyes remained still. She was lost in that thoughtful gaze, the gaze that meant something else was on in her mind.

Like Ella, she was probably wondering about Tobias's whereabouts. What was he doing? Where was he hiding? Who was he going to target next? And most importantly, was he looking for them? Did his contacts already have eyes on them in New Jersey, and if so, how long would it be before Tobias acted on his impulses? Ella wondered if this was the first time Mia had dealt with two serial killers at the same time.

No more secrets, she reminded herself.

"Ripley, is everything okay? You don't seem yourself."

The comment jolted Mia back to life. She skimmed the room, like she'd just woken up from a trance. She pulled her laptop closer and started typing, but said nothing.

"Ripley? I'm sorry Connor turned out to be a dud."

"Dark, just forget about it. And no, things are not okay."

Ella pushed it. If this concerned Tobias, she needed to know. "What's wrong? You can tell me. Has the director been in touch?"

"No, I can't tell you about it, because you'll take it to heart, and then it becomes my problem. We've got two serial killers on the loose and no whereabouts on either of them, so let me worry about the director and you worry about catching this asshole."

Ella said nothing and turned to the pile of paperwork on her desk. She waited for the tension to die down, then spread out the paperwork by victim. One side of the desk for Leslie Buddington, one for James Floyd. She first examined the crime scene photos to see if she'd missed any clues, but she'd already committed all of the graphic details to memory and had scoured them passively all day. Two lifeless bodies, cruelly murdered, and there was nothing on them to suggest who the culprit might be.

They had two links. One, they were both medical workers. Two, they were both in this strange photograph that James's wife had given them. They had officers checking out the people in the photograph, and judging by the report that came back, none of them could be their unsub. Ella still needed to check their alibis, but of the six remaining people, two no longer lived in the state, and all the others were at work the night of the murders. Given none of them were the unsub, Ella had officers staking out the care home. The employees had also been told to stay on high alert.

"What's going on with the workers at the care home?" Mia asked as though she'd read her mind.

Ella gave her the details. "The remaining four are working overnights for the next few nights, so we have two officers keeping an eye on the home. We'll still need to interview them when we have the chance."

Mia gave no response and went back to typing furiously. A little acknowledgment would have been nice, but Ella didn't want to irritate her partner further. She let it slide.

If their professional lives didn't get them anywhere, maybe the answer was in their personal lives. Ella opened up a browser tab and searched for *Doctor James Floyd Princeton.* Very little popped up, except an article about James receiving an award for his services. The same award Ella had seen in his home. She quickly scanned it but there was nothing of importance, except a photo of James on a fishing trip.

She searched for Leslie Buddington and found one or two social media pages, eerily bare for a woman of her age. Ella scrolled through what pictures she had available, finding a few selfies, a photo of her at a nightclub, and some scenic shots. By the looks of it, Leslie didn't post a whole lot, and she didn't seem to have a boyfriend or a partner. Her records showed that her parents lived in New York too, so it looked like Leslie was something of a loner.

Ella sat and stared at the wall, praying that her subconscious would make a connection her rational mind couldn't. She let the grays dissolve her vision until she was lost in a field of colorless fuzz. The first thing she saw was Mark's face, annoyingly handsome but concealing a lethal thirst for abuse. Then she heard his voice, soft and eloquent, but one she now associated with crippling insecurity.

Mark's image faded to Tobias Campbell's. Skinny, rat-like, yellow teeth behind thin lips. A bald head covered in scars. She imagined him nestled in her apartment parking lot, hiding among the communal trash bins, waiting for nightfall so he could slip into her building unseen. She quickly shook the thought away, then grabbed her phone and turned it back on. She needed to remind Jenna to lock the doors and windows whether she was in or out. Jenna was anything but thoughtful.

She hammered out a text message as more notifications from Mark flashed up, pinging in quick succession like a winning slot machine.

We need to talk.

Call me now.

Why are you making this so hard?

Ella ignored them and turned her phone off again. She caught Mia's eye as she looked up.

"Dark," Mia said and waited, as though she was finishing the question telepathically. "What's going on with you? You never turn your phone off."

"Too many distractions," Ella said.

"I know the feeling. If there's something else going on, please tell me. We've been through this."

Could Ella tell the truth about Mark? Add another issue to the growing pile? Mia and Mark had been colleagues for over a decade and Ella didn't want to sour it between them. This issue was between her and her ex-boyfriend, not Mark and Mia. She was going to do everything to keep it that way. Ella didn't want to share it with Mia because it didn't have anything to do with her. If the issue overspilled into her professional life, then she'd bring it up. Until then, it was her own problem to deal with.

"It's fine. I just really thought we were making headway but now I can't seem to figure anything out. I don't know where to start."

A knock at the door interrupted them. Chief Craven peered his head through. Ella was glad of the intrusion.

"Got something for you," Craven said. He dropped a stack of photographs on the table. Great, Ella thought, more paperwork to trawl through.

"What's this?" asked Ella.

"Photos of the possessions in James Floyd's car. The possessions themselves are with forensics, so pictures are all we have."

Ella quickly flipped through the photos. Fifteen pages of the car's interior and close-ups of various, everyday items. Probably not much here, she thought.

"How are things going?" Craven asked.

"Best not to ask," said Mia.

Craven took the hint and left without saying goodbye. Ella laid out the new photos, fast running out of desk space.

James Floyd seemed to have plenty of junk in his vehicle. A flask, receipts, tissues, a pile of business cards. Nothing that really told her a whole lot about this man. She idly scoured the close-up photos of the business cards.

A neurologist's professional card. An advertisement for a local builder. Repairmen. Car washing services.

Then she reached the last page and froze.

She blinked rapidly to clear the gunk from her eyes. It was a business card for a local therapist.

And not only that, but the name rang familiar.

Ethan Heroux.

Where had she heard that name before?

Ella moved back to the other piles and rapidly retraced her steps. She hadn't heard the name since she'd arrived at the precinct. Someone had mentioned it earlier, while she was on the road.

"A-ha," she said. The comment caught Mia's attention.

"Got something?"

"Not sure. Ethan Heroux," she repeated the name.

"Who's that?" asked Mia.

Ella was lost in the court transcript from Connor Jansen's trial. She sped through the text looking for the name.

Page 37. She found it.

"Oh damn," Ella said. "Ripley, look at this."

Mia jumped up from her seat and joined Ella on the other side of the desk. She glanced at the section Ella was pointing at. It was part of Leslie Buddington's testimony.

Leslie Buddington: "Working with Connor really affected me. I'm constantly on edge. I've been speaking with a therapist about it."

Defense attorney Riley: "A therapist? Would you say Connor's actions have prevented you from performing your job to your optimal ability?"

Leslie Buddington: "Very much so. My therapist says that witnessing this kind of trauma could have long term effects too."

Defense attorney Riley: "Who is your therapist?"

Leslie Buddington: "Doctor Ethan Heroux."

"Well, shit. They both saw the same therapist," Mia said. "But so what? That doesn't mean he has a vendetta against these people."

But there was something else. Something that ignited a spark in the back of her brain. She'd seen the name Heroux before. She jumped to her laptop and began searching. As the muscle memory kicked in, it suddenly came back to her.

"When we were in the hospital, I went into James Floyd's office. There was some paperwork there about a deceased patient." She closed her eyes and visualized the name on the paper. "Marcus Heroux."

Mia clasped her hands together. "Rookie, are you high? Did you seriously read a doctor's personal files? Without permission?"

"It was an accident," Ella said. "I just saw the words and the surname stuck in my head. You don't forget a surname like that."

Mia shook her head disappointingly but didn't question things further.

"Hey, you said this morning it was time we broke the rules a little," Ella said.

"Yeah, but not like this."

Ella pulled up Ethan Heroux's website. He was a middle-aged man, slick brown hair, thick-rimmed glasses. He wore a white turtleneck in his professional headshot.

PRINCETON PSYCHOTHERAPY CLINIC. A SAFE, JUDGMENT-FREE SPACE.

Ella scoured the site, not quite sure what she was looking for. She needed information, and she knew just the person to give it to her. She looted her pockets and found what she needed.

Ella turned her phone on for the second time, ignoring the old messages again. She dialed the number on the business card in front of her. Four rings, five rings.

"Hello?" a voice said.

"Kelly, it's Agent Dark. We met in your office earlier."

"Oh, hello again Miss Dark. What can I do for you?"

"I'm sorry to call you so late, but I just needed to ask you something." Ella didn't wait for an acknowledgement. "Do you know anyone named Ethan Heroux?"

"Yes I do. How do you know about him?"

Ella sensed a little tension down the line. She must have stumbled across something they shouldn't know about.

"His name came up in our investigation. We just wanted to clear him."

"I see. Ethan Heroux used to work for Princeton Hospital, but he's no longer affiliated with us."

Ella turned the phone to loudspeaker. "Why? Was he fired?"

"Once again Miss Dark, this is off the record. Heroux and the hospital directors had a falling out, but I don't see how this impacts your investigation."

"It's just a formality," Ella said, but couldn't shake the feeling there was something here. "Can you tell me what they fell out about? I assure you this will be kept confidential."

Kelly Adams went quiet for a moment. There was some scratching sounds down the phone line. Ella sensed movement on the other side. "His son was under hospital care but passed away. That's all I can really say."

A connection. A new avenue. She clenched her fist in triumph.

"Kelly, thank you for your help. I'll leave you to your evening." Ella hung up the phone, ran out of the room and found Chief Craven's office. He was scrawling something on his wall-to-floor whiteboard.

"Chief, can you pull up an address for me?" Ella asked. Mia appeared behind her.

70

"Can do. Name?"

"Ethan Heroux." Ella spelled it out for him.

"Dark, his address is on the business card."

"That's his work address. It's nearly 7pm. He'll be at home now."

"330 Aldgate Court, 8540," Craven said. "You finger this guy for something?"

Ella made a mental note. "We'll see." She turned to Ripley. "Are you coming?"

CHAPTER THIRTEEN

Ella filled in the gaps while Mia drove to the therapist's house.

"Leslie Buddington said in court that Heroux was her therapist. Police found Heroux's card in James Floyd's vehicle, and it had an appointment date written on the back. That means they both went to the same therapist."

Mia had avoided the main road in favor of side streets. At this hour, it got them there much quicker. Ella was going to suggest it anyway but she knew better than to give Mia driving advice.

"What was this about a son? I'm lost."

"Marcus Heroux. He died under hospital care. That's the documentation I found in James Floyd's desk. Maybe Ethan blames James and possibly Leslie for his son's death? Maybe his sessions helped him get closer to them? It seems too convenient to ignore."

"Here," Mia said. "330 Aldgate Court. Damn, this guy lived big."

Another grandiose house. A vast pebbled driveway around a water fountain. A row of stone pillars holding up the porch. Spotlights beaming from the roof onto the lawn that encircled the home. At the far end of the grass, Ella noticed a couple of horse stables. How the other half lived, she thought.

Mia dropped the car outside the gate. The agents stepped out and walked up the driveway. Ella felt like they were being watched. Surely a place like this had motion-detecting cameras somewhere.

They reached the doorway without any alarm bells going off. Ella banged on the door and saw a light in a downstairs room flick on. Something stirred behind the curtain. Someone was home.

A minute passed with no answer.

"Mr. Heroux, please open up," called Ella, unsure if her volume was high enough to reach the person inside. Ella knocked again to the same result.

"He's ducking us," Mia said, then smashed her own iron fists against the door. "Mr. Heroux, FBI, please open up."

The downstairs light flicked off. Ella heard voices, sobbing. She turned to Mia. She'd also heard it.

"Smells suspicious," Mia shouted. "Go nuclear."

Ella didn't need any further instruction. She pulled the door handle to the expected result, then shouldered the door with every ounce of strength she had. It rumbled in the frame and flared up her injury, but she shook off the pain and carried on. Ella stepped back, put all of her weight into her foot and launched it against the door handle.

It burst open, ripping the deadbolt completely off. "Mr. Heroux, please make yourself known." They ran down the extravagant hallway looking for entry into the room they'd seen the figure. One door led to the right. Ella grabbed the handle and pulled it but it was locked.

"Excuse me," a woman's voice screeched. "What do you think you're doing in my house?"

At the top of a spiraling stairway, a woman stood in a dressing robe and a towel around her head.

"We're looking for Ethan Heroux," Ella said. "Where is he?"

The woman ripped the towel off. "Who the hell do you think you are, breaking my door down? I oughta sue the backsides off you."

"FBI," Ella said. "Where is Ethan?"

The door beside her burst open and a red-faced gentleman stomped within spitting distance of Ella. "Here I am. I'm Ethan. Who in God's name are you? Why are you in my home?"

Ella prepared herself to fight. Ethan looked like a ball of rage and understandably so.

"Ethan, we're with the FBI. We need to talk with you about Leslie Buddington and James Floyd."

"I'm in the middle of a session, you fools." Behind Ethan, a young woman peered over his shoulder. She quickly retreated when she saw the commotion. "What's so important that you had to break into my house?"

Mia jumped in. "Your session is over. We need to talk with you urgently. Either we do it right here or we take you down to the precinct. The choice is yours."

"Come again? The precinct? You need to start making sense because I have no idea what you're talking about," Ethan shouted.

"Leslie and James. They were clients of yours, yes?" Mia said.

"Patient confidentiality, heard of it?" said Ethan. "I'm not telling you anything. I don't care who you are."

Ethan's wife rushed between Ella and her husband. "Oh my God. Are you trying to say Ethan is a murder suspect?" she asked.

"Murder? Okay, now you've completely lost me."

"I heard about it on the news earlier. You were still in session," the woman said to Ethan. "They were… clients of yours?"

Ethan fell against the wall behind him. A blank expression spread across his face, like he was staring into the abyss. "Someone hit the reset button, because I'm really lost here." He retreated into the room, leaving the agents and his wife in the hallway. A few seconds later, Ethan's client walked between them without saying a word, hopped over the broken door and escaped into the street.

"Okay, come in," Ethan said. "But you're paying for a new door." Ethan led the agents into his study.

***

Things calmed down, but Ella had a great suspicion that Ethan was hiding something. Something about this didn't seem right to her. He fit the psychological profile very well. He wasn't physically imposing, he was likely familiar with the layout of Princeton Hospital and possibly Tower Lodge Care Home, and he was smart enough to grasp certain medical concepts.

There were only two chairs in the room. Ethan sat on one, Mia on the other. Ella leaned against the door in case Ethan tried to make a daring escape.

"Honestly, I don't know about any murders," Ethan said.

"You don't watch the news? None of your colleagues told you? It seems odd that someone of your status wouldn't immediately be alerted of these deaths," Ella said.

Ethan shrugged. "No I don't watch the news. The past few days, I haven't had time to go to the bathroom, let alone read about local crime. What happened, exactly?"

"A young girl named Leslie Buddington was found dead in her car outside Tower Lodge Care Home. I believe you're familiar with her, right?"

Ethan's face turned pale. "Of course. She was a patient of mine. Leslie is dead?"

Ella concentrated on nothing but Ethan's micro signals. His demeanor stayed consistent. He leaned forward as if to say *I'm not hiding anything.* So far, she couldn't fault him, but psychopaths were experts at playing the part they needed to.

"Yes. Dead. Stabbed, kept alive, and strangled to death."

Ethan held up a palm in a time-out gesture. "Excuse me. I think I'm going to be sick." He reached over and drank a glass of water. "I assure you, I have nothing to do with this."

Ella didn't acknowledge his declaration of innocence just yet. She continued with the facts. "And then there's Doctor James Floyd. You know him too, I believe."

"I do. Fantastic doctor. Fantastic man. Please don't tell me…"

"I'm afraid so," Mia said. "Found dead outside Princeton Hospital. Stabbed, resuscitated multiple times, and then strangled. How do you feel about that?"

Ethan cupped his face with both hands. His breathing sped up. A genuine display of emotion or a futile attempt to hide the truth, Ella thought.

"Now, we heard that you no longer work for Princeton Hospital. Can you tell us about that?" Ella asked.

Ethan took his time. Ella used the opportunity to scope his body language.

"I never worked for them," Ethan said. "If anyone told you that then it's miscommunication. I was a partner of theirs. That's all."

Ella wasn't quite sure what that involved. "Partner? Explain."

"I'm a therapist. I specialize in trauma, grief, loss. Princeton asked me to become their affiliated therapist for any staff members who had mental health struggles. Obviously, doctors have to deal with a lot of traumas. Sometimes, they'd send patients to me to help them out. That's all we ever were."

Made sense, Ella thought, but it was still a coincidence that both Leslie and James came to this same person.

"And Leslie and James both had troubles?"

"My lips are sealed. Even in death, I believe in confidentiality. Please respect that."

Mia this time. "One of our sources said that you and the Princeton directors had a falling out. Can you shed some light on that?"

Ethan shook his head. "A falling out? Where did that come from? We never fell out."

"No?" asked Mia.

"No. I simply told them I couldn't take on any more patients. As well as dealing with their staff, I have plenty of my own clients. My calendar was full, and Princeton wanted to pile more work on me. I told them I couldn't handle it. If I did, I'd be stretching myself too thin. This was around six months ago, and they didn't renew my contractor status with them."

That hellish disappointment came hurling back. The more Ethan talked, the less likely he seemed of being their unsub. Something in his tone and his attitude suggested he was telling nothing but the truth.

"Okay. What about your son?" Ella asked.

Ethan kept his composure but the word stirred something behind his eyes. Tears welled in his eyelids. Suddenly, she regretted mentioning it. Even if Ethan had something to hide, it was undoubtedly a terrible subject to bring up.

"Marcus passed away in hospital. Peacefully. He was 21 years old."

Ella couldn't hold the sympathy back. "I'm very sorry to hear that."

"Thank you. As a grief counselor, I've come to terms with it, but it's very hard as you can understand."

Ella quickly figured out a way to address the subject without sounding accusatory. "Was Marcus under the care of James Floyd?"

"No," Ethan said, as though it was common knowledge. "James had no involvement. Neither did Leslie, if that's what you're thinking. Marcus was under the care of Doctor Gerritsen."

The finish line sped away, far out of her grip. First Connor Jansen yielded nothing, now this. She did her best to hide her disappointment but she knew it was plastered all over her face. All the questions she had abruptly vanished.

"What happened to Marcus was unavoidable," Ethan said. "I'm at ease with it. Nothing short of a miracle could have saved him. I don't hold any resentment towards his carers at all. They did everything they could."

Mia took over. "Can you verify your whereabouts on the nights of April 30 and May 3?" she asked.

Ethan scratched his cheek and glanced at the ceiling. "What time?"

"Between midnight and 1am."

"I was working on the basement. Renovating it. Ask my wife."

Ella's mind went to James and Leslie's therapy sessions. What could they have talked about? What were their troubles? She had to find a way to get this information out of Ethan, confidentiality be damned.

"Did James and Leslie come to you directly, or were they referred to you by someone else?" Ella asked. "Maybe someone who was concerned for their wellbeing."

Ethan folded his arms, a gesture of defense. "They came to me directly." He punctuated with the sentence with a heavy cough. "Well, my wife was the catalyst. She worked with Leslie and saw she was struggling."

"Their professions took a mental toll on them, then."

"I'm afraid I can't say any more. What we talk about in here stays in here. It's my ethos."

"Mr. Heroux, those two clients are dead and we're trying to find out who killed them. If they revealed anything that could indicate why someone might want to kill them, we need to know about it," Ella said.

Ethan deflected the comment. "I don't know what you want me to say. Nothing springs to mind. They had problems, just like everyone else."

"Personal or professional?" she asked.

"A little of both."

"Mr. Heroux, we sat with James's wife, drinking herself to oblivion. I sat at James's empty desk. I found a necklace he kept from an old patient he felt close to. As far as we can see, he was an absolute saint. If we're missing something, something we can dig into, we're desperate to find it. You might be the only person in the world with that information."

Ethan took another drink of water. He ran his finger around the rim of the glass and then placed it down slowly.

"Alright. But this stays between us. You don't repeat this to anyone."

"You have our word," Mia said. Ella nodded in agreement.

"Both Leslie and James, they had the same problem. A problem not exclusive to medical officials by any means, but certainly magnified by their profession."

"What problem was this?" Ella asked.

"Recurrent anticipatory grief."

Familiar words, but not a term Ella recognized. "Can you explain what that is? I don't know."

Ethan folded his arms again, reverting to therapist mode. "It's the distress a person feels in the days or weeks before the death of a loved one or any other impending loss. It's the experience of knowing that a change is coming, and starting to experience bereavement in the face of that knowledge."

Ella remembered all of her interviewees saying how James Floyd often forged close relationships with his patients, not to mention he'd saved a keepsake from one of them. James obviously forged great bonds with those he cared for.

"James and Leslie struggling with the loss of their patients?"

"Yes. Both of them were highly sensitive individuals, very in tune with their emotions. To people like that, dealing with constant death, even in a professional setting, was like a slow-acting poison to their mental health. James dealt with a lot of end-of-life patients; Leslie worked in a care home where turnover was regular. Put simply, they struggled with the cruel notion of mortality."

"Don't we all," Mia said.

Ethan looked a little offended. "I'm sure you deal with your fair share of death, agents, but with all due respect, you don't connect with the victims in the same way doctors and carers do. Bodies show up as bodies to you. To people like James and Leslie, those bodies were once living beings."

Ella wished it was that easy. "Understood, Mr. Heroux. Thank you for being honest with us."

Mia passed her card to Ethan and prepared to leave. "If you think of anything else, please let us know."

Ella gave her thanks to the therapist. He wasn't their unsub. Defeated, she and Mia took their leave, walking over the broken front door.

"We'll get this fixed for you," said Ella.

"Please do."

They reached the car. Ella had had enough for one day. There was only so much disappointment one person could take and she'd reached her limit.

"Hotel?" Mia asked.

"Please. You?"

"Yeah, I'm done. Let's rest."

And as if Ella didn't have enough on her mind, now she had to survive the night.

CHAPTER FOURTEEN

When Ella and Mia arrived at their hotel for the night, Ella asked the question she'd been dreading.

"Ripley, could we share a room tonight?"

Mia leaned on the counter and pushed the service bell. "Yeah. I was going to suggest that anyway. It's probably safer for both of us."

A clerk arrived to take their details. Ella passed over her company credit card and requested a double room. The clerk summoned an orderly to take their bags but Mia insisted they do it themselves.

"Paranoid?" Ella asked.

"Can't be too careful, especially right now."

"Good thinking." Ella was too tired to even consider that Tobias might have followers in this backdoor motel, but he'd had people watching her in both Baltimore and Delaware, so it wasn't unreasonable. She hauled her bag to the first floor and found their room. Mia swiped it open.

The room was almost a carbon copy of the last one she'd been in. She was starting to understand that life on the road was a recurring series of the exact same sights and smells as the last place, just with a different two letters after the city name. If someone asked her what state was she in right now, she'd have to think twice about it. She remembered an interview with the guitarist from Guns 'N' Roses, a notorious hater of traveling. *When someone asks me if I saw much of Paris, I point to the hotel walls and say 'this is what I saw of Paris.'*

Two single beds took up most of the floor space, and there was a small dressing table, a chair, and a TV attached to the wall. She took the bed closest to the bathroom, because ever since her troubles with Mark began, she found herself peeing a hell of a lot more in the night. Whether it was related to her troubles or whether it was age catching up with her, she couldn't be sure.

"You don't snore, do you?" Mia asked.

"No, I have a technique," Ella said.

"Of course you do. Does it work?"

"Actually, I have no idea. It's been ages since I slept with somebody. In the same room, I mean."

79

"I know what you meant. Well I'll let you know in the morning. I don't have a technique myself so plug your ears." Mia shamelessly threw her clothes on the nearby chair and jumped into bed. Ella only wished she had that much confidence.

"7am, bright and early?" Ella asked.

"Always. Sleep well."

Ella got ready for bed, a ritual that included deleting all her phone notifications. The last thing she wanted was to wake up to an overload of messages. She turned the light out, climbed into bed and turned on her phone. The messages she'd ignored earlier all popped up, a whopping 14 of them.

Where are you? Who are you with?

What case are you on?

I'm working a serial and I need your help.

We need to talk.

Call me now.

Why are you making this so hard?

Repeat ad infinitum. She scrolled through her conversation screen with Mark, seeing endless messages all of a similar format. Short, vague messages that tried to manipulate her into contacting him. How many texts would it take before he finally got the message? More than a million, by the looks of things.

She got severe déjà vu from her case in Delaware. Down there, she'd promised herself she wouldn't take any more of Mark's toxic behavior. She'd promised she'd break it off with him and give him a dose of cruel truth. Worst of all, she'd done exactly that, and he simply hadn't accepted it. When she got back home, it was time to go full sledgehammer. Or nuclear as Ripley would say. She was a damn FBI agent for God's sake. She'd brought down some of the most sadistic psychopaths America had to offer. How hard was it to give Mark the same treatment she'd shown the Gemini killer? Or the Mad Coin Collector as the press were now calling her recent catch?

Ella thought about deleting all his messages but decided against it. She needed proof of his actions in case it ever came to her word against his. Evidence was everything in this game.

Lying on her side and staring at her screen, only now did she realize she hadn't texted her roommate back home. She quickly hammered out a message, reminding Jenna to lock the doors and windows. She also told Jenna that if one of her multiple lovers was staying over, put his shoes outside the door. It was a trick she'd learned interviewing battered woman during her time at Virginia police. Women who put men's boots outside their door were less likely to be targeted by an attacker. Serial killing sometimes came with sexist undertones, something that made the whole thing that little bit sadder.

She closed her eyes but sleep felt a million miles away. Her brain was rampant with activity and it would take hours for it to die down. She thought of the most mundane things she could; being stuck in traffic, junk mail, TV shopping channels, golf.

None of it seemed to do the trick.

How long would it take a person to get from Maine to New Jersey? Or Maine to Washington, D.C.? Three hours? Could Tobias be in either state right now, hunting high and low for the people he desired the most? Or was lying low in Maine, figuring out his next move?

What if Tobias had contacts in the airline industry that could smuggle him wherever he wanted to go? Or what if he just drove the whole journey? Nine hours, ten at most.

The ideas woke her up even more. Sleep was even further out of her grip. She decided to clear her head and focus on absolutely nothing, but then the pillow became too hot. She needed the bathroom. An empty head meant you were more aware of your senses and that brought its own problems.

She got up, stumbled around in the dark and found her way to the bathroom. When she got back, she saw a light on Mia's side of the room. Ella worried that her stumbling had woken her partner.

"Sorry, I didn't mean to disturb you," Ella whispered.

Mia turned the light on Ella. "No apology necessary. I'm still up. Been catching up on emails."

Ella got back into bed and sat up. "Any news?"

"Nothing," Mia said sternly. "He's vanished like a ghost in the fog. Gone. They've checked every CCTV camera within ten miles and haven't seen a single thing."

Ella lay back against the headboard and stared into the darkness. The longer he stayed invisible, the more she felt responsible for what might happen. "How is that even possible?" she asked.

"I don't know, but Houdini this guy ain't. He's flesh and blood like everyone else. He has to be somewhere. He has to surface eventually. He can't have just disappeared into the void."

There was something Ella wanted to know, and for several months, she'd never had the balls to bring it up. But if there was a better time than now, Ella didn't know it.

"Ripley, can I ask you something about your past? Something I know you don't like discussing."

Mia's phone light disappeared, sending the room into pure blackness. "You want to know how I first caught him, don't you?"

"Yes."

Mia had only given Ella the short version every time she'd asked. Sure, Ella had studied the case to obsessive levels and devoured the FBI files on the case, but hearing the details from the horse's mouth was unbeatable. The only problem was that the case was still as traumatic for Mia today as it was 16 years ago.

"It started in 2001, if I remember rightly. A place called Mount Carroll about ten miles outside of Chicago." Mia lay down in bed and spoke towards the ceiling. "We were called in to investigate a string of suicides. Four women had been found hanging from trees out in the Illinois countryside."

Ella already knew these details but she didn't interrupt. She was shocked Mia actually obliged her request to tell her story.

"We thought maybe there was something in the water. Something driving these women to suicide. When we looked more closely, we found the women killed themselves under suspicious circumstances. We found secondary fingerprints on one of the nooses."

"That's when you realized they were murders?"

"Not completely. A fifth incident followed not long after, but this time, a CCTV camera caught the whole thing on tape. What we saw was… well, I'd never seen anything like it. It wasn't brutal or gory, just… surreal. Like a silent horror movie from the twenties."

Ella had heard about the footage but had never seen it for herself. Rumor around the office was that it was locked in the deepest recesses of the evidence vault in Quantico, having only been viewed once in court. Ella once asked the archivist at HQ about it and he said it did indeed exist, and was labeled 'never to be viewed, duplicated, or deleted.'

"Two people sat on some grass beside a tree, a noose between them. One was a girl, and you could see her face clearly. The other had this bizarre mask on, like one of those plague doctor masks. They talked for about five minutes, like two old friends. The masked guy put his hand on hers, then she started crying. Then the woman just picked up the noose and hanged herself while the masked guy watched."

Ella winced at the thought. Under other circumstances, she'd give anything to see the footage for herself. But now she was so close to the man in the plague doctor mask, she'd see it in a completely different light.

"That's when we knew they were serial killings. We started calling him the Executioner, and it took us four years to track him down. No more women died in that time, at least none that were officially attributed to him. But the chances of him going cold? Absolute zero. He killed a lot of others, and we had it on good authority that he'd tried his hand at child murder too. We actually found a plague doctor mask at the bottom of a well, and there was some DNA belonging to a missing 11-year-old girl on it."

That was the coldest part of all, Ella thought. She'd knowingly stood within ten feet of a man who'd taken the lives of innocent youngsters. If she could go back in time, she'd have smuggled a gun into Maine Prison and shot him through the heart the first chance she had.

"I traced the evidence to a little shack in the middle of the woods. We were worried the unsub was onto us, so I foolishly jumped right in, trying to be the hero of the day. I got to the shack alone and that's when I found... everything."

"What was in there?"

"Enough evidence to incriminate the owner on thirty-plus murders. Bloody nooses, I.D. cards, wallets, locks of hair, driving licenses, and the worst thing of all."

Ella already knew what it was. "Shoes."

"Shoes. Heels, boots, even tiny children's shoes. I was sick to my stomach because I knew exactly what it meant. I'd found the most prolific serial killer since Bundy or Dahmer. Then someone attacked me from the dark. He restrained me and dragged me into the woods. Stupidly, I told him backup was coming, and that just made everything worse."

Ella stayed silent and let Mia finish. Mia was giving her a lot more details than she'd anticipated. Maybe it was therapeutic for her, to finally talk about all this after such a long time.

"He beat me, gave me head trauma. He doused his shack in gasoline then sat down with me, just like he'd done with the girl in the video. He made *me* throw the match inside. I had to watch all the evidence inside burn to ashes. He knew exactly what he was doing. He was giving me a punishment worse than death, because he knew I could never prove what I saw."

"He made you doubt yourself," Ella said.

"Yes he did. Luckily, my partner at the time arrived and took the man down. He went willingly. There was no wild shootout or dramatic showdown. He just surrendered because he knew he'd prolonged his game-playing by doing what he did."

"What about the evidence?" Ella asked.

"Forensics found no traces of shoes. No I.D. cards. No nooses. Nothing. The defense said I was traumatized and that I hallucinated it all. Blamed the head trauma. That's when the FBI sent me to therapy. I'm certain I saw it, but professionals have told me otherwise. No modern serial killer could be responsible for thirty-plus deaths, not in this era of surveillance and DNA testing. That's what they said. They had the nerve to say this to *me*."

"I'm sorry, but thank you for telling me all this. I appreciate it."

"That's when we found out who he was. Keep in mind at this point, we didn't even know the guy's name. We couldn't find any identification on him. We still haven't, to this day. We found no records of his life. No employment history, no registered vehicles. He was like a supernatural phantom who only existed to kill. Tobias Campbell might not even be his real name."

This was a chapter Mia had tried to leave in the past, but Ella had resurrected it, rewritten it and made it even more harrowing than before.

"This is my fault," Ella said. "I baited him. I brought the Executioner back."

"No, he was always there in the background. I've been dealing with Tobias's shit long before I met you," Mia said. "Every year on my birthday, he sent me shoes. Tried to goad me into visiting him. I never gave in."

"But now you have to, because of me."

"Oh, I'm not giving in. If anything, this is the perfect excuse. If I met Tobias in prison, I couldn't exactly do anything other than talk. But if we meet on the streets, it's a different story. This needed to happen eventually, you just sped it all up. And don't worry, I won't let anything happen to you. We might have had our problems, but the past is the past. From now on it's me and you, no phantoms. Got it?"

Ella appreciated the rose-tinted excuse, but knew it wasn't completely true. Suddenly, the tiredness hit her now that she felt a little safer.

"Thanks Ripley. I won't let anything happen to you either."

"Appreciated. Now get to sleep. Who knows what tomorrow might bring?"

CHAPTER FIFTEEN

Anderson Cooper poured a tall glass of wine and collapsed in his chair. What was retirement if not an excuse to drink every night? He'd wake up tomorrow morning with a dreadful hangover, but unlike his med school days, he could take as long as he needed to nurse himself back to health.

He flicked through the TV channels, punctuating every channel switch with a flick of the wrist. Saturday nights were the worst for TV, but it meant he didn't have to think too much. The last thing he wanted right now was something heavy, so a celebrity panel show seemed an adequate choice.

Local news had been dominated by the murder of James Floyd. They'd spared some of the finer details, but the headline was clear as day: local doctor slayed outside workplace. Then there'd been the young girl too. Anderson didn't understand this world anymore; thank heavens he'd left the public arena when he had. Now all he had to worry about was what activities could keep him occupied throughout the week. Sometimes he missed the prestige that came with the old job, but at 62, he was lucky enough to call it a day while he still had a good few years left.

Anderson hadn't even unpacked his groceries. He'd just left them on the table for another time. One of the many benefits of not having women or children in the house. In some ways, he reveled in the minor chaos, like he was making up for years spent being overly sanitary.

Half a bottle of wine down, Anderson felt his eyes growing heavy. He let sleep come in small doses, using the volume of the TV to keep himself half-awake. Then everything went silent for a few minutes, and when he woke up, he realized he'd been out for almost half an hour.

It was still too early. He couldn't sleep yet because he'd just wake up at 4am ready to go. He took another dose of wine to prop him back up then rose to his feet. The murders were the first thing he thought of, and so Anderson went around his house locking all of the doors. Front, back, basement. He even ventured into the basement for the first time in a long time and made sure all the doors in there were bolted shut. Then he returned upstairs, went to the bathroom and sat on the throne. Sure, sitting down to do your business was emasculating but there was no one around to tell him so anymore. Plus it was much more comfortable than standing. His old legs couldn't carry the kind of weight they used to.

When he finished, he walked into his dusty old office and scanned the bookshelf. Maybe something here would help pass the rest of the night. The top three rows were all medical books, mostly for show when he brought guests here. He bent down to the bottom rows where the fiction was hiding and browsed the names on the spines. Some crime fiction, murder mysteries and the like. He laughed off the idea. That was the last thing he wanted right now, considered what happened to his old friend Floydy. He settled on some historical fiction, a Wild West saga about an outlaw on the hunt for a notorious oil baron. Anderson remembered starting the series years ago, so maybe now was the right time to finish it.

Then Anderson heard a sound from downstairs.

For a second, he remembered his old life, with a wife, two children and enough dogs to pull a sled. His first thought was that one of the mutts had tail-whipped an ornament, but there were no mutts anymore. Nothing but him and ten rooms of empty space.

He froze still for a moment, listening for anything that suggested life. Hissing pipes, neighbors arguing, external sounds that felt closer than they actually were.

It all stopped. Dead silence again.

Anderson felt a little relieved. Must have been his tired brain playing tricks on him, he thought. He went back downstairs, but as he reached his hallway, something was different.

Usually, the lamplight from the lounge illuminated the whole downstairs area, but everything had suddenly grown dim.

Of course, Anderson realized. The fuse must have blown in the light. "God dammit," he muttered under his breath. He hated messing around with electricity, especially at his age. One wrong move could mean a nasty accident.

Anderson felt his way around the room, bashing his knee against his sofa. He cursed again, but then he saw the blinking light on the TV. His router still flashed green and blue. If a fuse had blown downstairs, it always took out the whole floor.

His hand found the light switch in panic. He began to tremble. Something felt eerily off about this whole thing. It didn't make sense.

Anderson turned on the light. An orange glow engulfed the room, and Anderson saw that the room was not as he left it. There was one major difference.

"Hello, Mr. Cooper," the figure said.

Anderson dropped the book and recoiled against the wall. His hands darted towards the nearest heavy object but found nothing of the sort.

"Whoa now, who are you? Why are you in my house?"

The figure was wearing all black with a hood concealing his face. His hands were stuffed in the pockets of his jacket.

"I've been waiting a long time for this," the figure said. His voice was light, nasally, and unfamiliar. What few glimpses he caught of the intruder's face, he didn't recognize the features. This man was a stranger.

"Get out of here before I call the police," Anderson yelled. If he could dominate the confrontation, he might have a chance of scaring the intruder off. He continued to back away but found himself against the solid walls of the hallway. He could run upstairs, but there was no way out up there.

"You won't have time for that," said the intruder as he stepped closely. The man pulled one hand out of his pockets to reveal a gleaming silver blade. A butcher's knife, speckled with reddish blotches. Anderson recognized the image. He'd seen enough surgical tools with dried blood on them in his time. His thoughts turned to the recent murders, two in three days. The locals had told to be on high alert, but these things didn't happen to people like him.

Anderson had no choice, he realized. It was fight or flee, and he couldn't compete with someone wielding a blade. He turned and ran to the stairs, but the figure was next to him, breathing the same confined air as he was. Anderson toppled against the staircase, turned onto his back and furiously kicked, but there was no energy to draw on. The air left his body in a single torrential wave, leaving him breathless and immobile at the attacker's mercy. Only when he looked down did he see the butcher's knife buried deep in his stomach.

He didn't have the willpower to fight or move or even think. Anderson grabbed onto the banister in a final act of defiance, but there was nothing left inside of him. His vision went static, fuzzy, obscured. Shapes blurred into one another and the world became an unidentifiable, colorless mass.

But for a brief second, his awareness came surging back, and it might have been his brain accepting his oncoming fate, but he was sure he saw something familiar. Something he'd seen more times than he could count.

His attacker, now with his hood down and a sadistic grin on his face, was clutching a red medical tube.

CHAPTER SIXTEEN

Footsteps woke her up.

They weren't Ripley's. They were heavier and more carless. Ella stepped out of her bed. The lights from passing cars outside their window cast orange squares against the curtains, hypnotically dashing right to left.

Outside was still dark, so it must have been the middle of the night. She never woke early, unless something interrupted her. Maybe it was Ripley, pottering around, getting ready early?

No. It wasn't Ripley. Ella knew her rhythm. Shadows moved and danced against the far wall, but something told her that those shadows didn't belong to Ripley. She wasn't sure how she knew. Partner's intuition, maybe, the same way she could tell when Ripley was angry or irritated or focused. They had a different presence, an alien aura.

Ella feigned sleep but kept one eye open. The shadows melted off the walls and manifested right in front of her, lightly treading between her and Ripley's beds.

She only caught a glimpse, but there was enough to tell her that she was right. There was someone else in their room. She suddenly felt sick and dizzy. There was an icy chill in her fingertips.

Then the darkness consumed her. For a few seconds she saw nothing except brief flashes of light, but when her eyes adjusted to the room's conditions, she saw the outline of a man holding a knife in his hand. He was standing over Ripley as she slept. Ella tried to scream, but no sound came out. She jumped out of bed and tried to run towards him, but she was locked in place. The intruder didn't even notice Ella, focussing only on her partner. All she could do was watch.

In a series of violent thrusts, the figure plunged the knife into the heart of her sleeping partner. The sudden attack rendered Mia completely motionless. She couldn't struggle or fight back or make an escape. She was at the stranger's mercy.

Ella managed to escape her bed, but then froze in place, as though her feet were nailed to the ground. Then, everything came in small fragments, as though the picture had been smashed to pieces and she was assembling the jigsaw back together. Blood seeped from the bed onto the carpet. Ripley screamed at Ella to get out of the motel. The attacker turned around, pulled down his hood to reveal a strange mask. Two huge eyes, a long beak. The Executioner was here. Leaving her partner in a bloody heap, he launched towards Ella with his blade pointed towards her.

Her heart stopped beating. Her throat became agonizingly dry. She was on her side again, back in bed, one leg much colder than the other. Reality came crushing back, and she suddenly aware that she was looking at the back of her eyelids.

She opened her eyes, adjusting to focus on the curtains a few feet away. A trickle of sunlight seeped through. She sat up in bed and grabbed her phone off the table beside her. 6:30am. Only now did she realize that this masked intruder existed in her dreamworld, not in reality.

Ella shot up, embracing the chill of the room. The nightmare had made her heartbeat shoot up to an unhealthy 90bmp according to her watch. She wiped the sweat off her head and lay back down on her side.

Awaking to a dead body was a nightmare she'd had many times before, but the body was always her father's. In the 25 years she'd been experiencing it, it had never been anyone else. Maybe, all of the recent ordeals had overtaken her dad's death as the primary source of trauma in her life?

Ella double-checked the time, finding more notifications than she had 6 hours ago. Apparently Mark was already awake or he'd been texting her all night. Judging by the time he'd sent the messages; 2am, 4am, 5am, it was the latter.

You've gone to sleep without texting me. Are you for real?
You better be alone right now.
Reply as soon as you get this, or something bad will happen to you.

The messages were becoming interchangeable now, but the last one really caught her attention. It was a direct threat, something Mark hadn't done before. He'd scolded her, aggressively questioned her, and made baseless accusations, but he'd never threatened her with anything.

Emotional abuse was one thing, but physical abuse was a different ballpark. She'd thought that maybe he slapped her because of the heat of the moment, but it was quickly becoming clear that Mark had every intention to hurt her. She didn't know what was worse, Tobias Campbell or Mark Balzano. At least she understood Tobias to an extent. He was a merciless psychopath who got off on manipulation and cruelty, but Mark was supposed to be an FBI agent. Just like every other agent, he took an oath to uphold the law when he started the

Bureau. How could he be a hero in one breath and a monster in another? She couldn't get into his head at all. What was his end game here? To get back with Ella so he could continually abuse her?

Maybe he had abandonment issues. Whatever it was, it wasn't her problem anymore. If he wanted a fight, he was going to damn well get it. The next time she saw him, she was going to give him what he needed, and it wasn't a sit-down conversation. If she had to bloody him up, so be it. If she had to stomp some sense into him with her own boots, so be it. There was only so much a person could take and she hit that limit a long time ago.

"Dark, you up?" Ripley called, appearing behind her like a phantom.

Ella quickly dropped her phone down the side of the bed. She really didn't want Mia to see Mark's messages. Not only did she want to keep this between her and Mark, but telling Ripley about it felt akin to telling the teacher about your home life. She still wanted to main a work-life balance, and her relationship with Mark fell outside of work boundaries.

"I am. Are you?" Ella asked. She recognized how stupid the comment was as soon as it left her mouth.

"Yeah, but I wish I wasn't. There's no pleasant way to wake up in New Jersey."

Ella laughed out of acknowledgment, but she liked this state. It looked nice and the people were accommodating. What more could she ask for? "Suit yourself. It seems alright here."

"You'll learn. I'd rather be dead in Washington than alive in New Jersey. Did you get any sleep at all?"

Ella peered in the opposite direction to give Mia some privacy, but she saw in her peripherals that she was already dressed.

"Not a whole lot but enough. You got ready quickly."

"Early morning. Seedy motel. Muscle memory nearly had me slipping out of here before you woke up."

"Ha. You didn't snore by the way, if you're wondering."

"Neither did you, but you fidgeted like hell. If we were in the same bed I would have kicked you."

Must have been the nightmares. Now that Ella thought about it, sometimes she'd go to sleep on one side of the bed and wake up on the other. She just assumed it was normal.

"I do that. What do we have on the agenda for today?"

"No agenda. That's the best thing about this job. But since we're early, why don't we get breakfast somewhere? I'm in the mood for something dirty. Something bacony."

Ella's appetite had completely vanished in recent weeks. She couldn't remember the last time she ate something that wasn't straight out of the fridge. Maybe something heavy would do her good. "Sounds like a plan. Then how about we head to the precinct and start looking at these victims again? I think we could…"

A humming phone interrupted her speech. It wasn't hers. Ripley grabbed her bag off the floor and scoured the contents. "It's six-thirty. Who the hell is calling me now?"

The idea of someone calling Mia so early rattled her. It couldn't be HQ because no one was there yet. She had it on good authority that the director didn't sleep until 3am every night, so the chances of him being up already were minimal.

"No number. Great," Ripley said. She answered the call, then Ella watched her expression change from annoyance to distress. The two agents locked eyes, and Ripley gave that familiar disappointed smile.

"Understood," Mia said. "See you there."

Ella didn't comment, just waited for the bad news.

"When and where?" she asked.

"Last night. At home."

Breakfast would have to wait.

CHAPTER SEVENTEEN

This one wasn't like the others, Mia thought.

She and Ella stood in the home of Anderson Cooper, a local man in his sixties according to Chief Craven. The house was spacious but not well-maintained. It hadn't been vacuumed in a long while and dusted coated most of the surfaces. Mia could say for certain that no woman had lived here for a while.

But the real focus was the dead body lying on the staircase. Equally concerning was the medical tube sprouting from his lacerated stomach. The poor man lay in a pool of his own blood, white eyeballs and all. A forensic officer swabbed the corpse while Mia, Ella, and Craven watched from a distance.

"What do we know about him?" Mia asked.

"Anderson Cooper. Doctor Anderson Cooper, to be precise. Sixty-two years old." Craven said.

"Another doctor?" she asked. The link was there, too present to be ignored. Yet another medical official slain. They were dealing with someone who had a vendetta against the medical community.

"A neurologist, but he retired last year apparently," Craven said. "Imagine that. Retiring only to be stabbed to death a year later. Life's a cruel mistress sometimes."

"Did he work at Princeton Hospital?" Ella asked.

"No. Locum. Freelance," Craven said.

"Who called it in?" Mia asked.

"Neighbor. Heard the screams last night but thought nothing of it. When she saw his trash cans weren't on the curb this morning, she knew something was wrong. Apparently Anderson was as punctual as it came. That's when she called us and well, here we are."

"He was one of *those* types," Mia said. "Always the first one up. Poor guy. Well, this is different than the others. Our unsub has jammed that medical tube right in the wound. That's new." She turned to her partner, who looked as perplexed as she'd ever seen her. "Dark? Thoughts?"

The forensic officer took their last photographs and passed them by with a nod. It was their signal they could inspect the body. Ella moved closer, bent down and examined the victim's stomach. She looked like she was about to wretch.

"He's getting a taste for this now," Ella said.

Mia thought the same but she wanted to know Ella's thought pattern. "How do you figure?"

"This isn't stalking in a parking lot. He invaded this guy's home. He wanted privacy so he could do… this. He wanted to savor it, make the most of it. This isn't some random attack, this is a targeted homicide."

Mia followed the blood spatter. It began on the staircase and ended in the hallway. The whole attack took place here. "Did Anderson have any family?" she asked.

"Divorced, but he has two kids. They're both at college in New York. His ex-wife lives a million miles away too."

"Why would someone want to kill a retired neurologist?" Ella asked.

"Easy target maybe?" asked Craven. "Don't think of me as insensitive, but a guy like this isn't going to put up much of a fight. I've seen more muscles on a seafood platter."

"No," Mia said. "This is the third medical worker in four days. There's no chance our killer would risk breaking into someone's home if he just wanted to kill any old doctor. There's a reason he chose Anderson."

"Speaking of breaking in," Craven said, "that's something we haven't figured out yet. We had to bash the doors down to get in here. It was locked six ways from Sunday."

"He could have climbed in through a window, or befriended Anderson at the door. He might have genuinely been friends with Anderson. We can't rule anything out yet."

Mia joined her partner at the foot of the body and eyed it top to bottom. One deep laceration in the chest and one medical tube inserted in. No other wounds and no ligature marks.

"One stab wound just like the others."

"No strangulation this time," Ella said. "No injures to the neck. He just left him like this to die."

"We both know he didn't leave while Anderson was alive," Mia said.

Ella nodded, distressed. "Yeah. He watched him die." Ella fell silent while she took close-up photographs of Anderson's body, focusing mostly on the area around the tube. Mia knew that look. Ella had something on her mind.

"Dark, right now would be a great time for one of your crazy theories, because honestly, I'm staring at a wall here. Maybe I'm just tired, but I can't crack this guy's head at all. I couldn't tell you what he wants or what he's trying to say."

Ella pocketed her phone. "Let me think. There's something here, I can feel it. Something we're missing."

"We've got a young woman, a middle-aged man and an older man. The victimology is all over the place. The killing methods have varied. He injected one with chemicals. He attacks people in their cars and homes and in parking lots. If it wasn't for the tubes and the time frame, these could easily be classed as separate incidents."

Craven interrupted. "We've got the neighbor outside if you wanna talk to her," he said.

Mia left the scene, made her way through Anderson's home to the front door. It was hanging on by one hinge after the battering from the police. Just outside on the doorstep stood an elderly woman in a purple coat and hair so white she reminded Mia of a wizard. She looked like she'd seen a ghost.

"Hi, are you the neighbor who called the police?" Mia asked.

The old woman nodded. "Yes. Please miss, what happened to old Cooper? He was my best friend."

Mia needed the rookie. She was the sympathy-giver out of the two. "I'm sorry, but he passed away last night. Please accept my condolences."

"Passed away? Dead? You mean he got killed?"

Mia didn't have the energy to beat around the bush. The truth was always best. "Yes he did, ma'am. I'm sorry I had to be the one to tell you."

The old woman whose name she didn't even know suddenly embraced her. She buried her head against Mia's neck, and Mia had no choice but to gently hold her. Suddenly, Ella appeared behind them. Mia gave her a nod, as if to say *this is your territory.*

"Miss, we're very sorry to hear about Anderson's passing," Ella jumped in, "but maybe you could help us catch whoever did this."

The old woman unearthed herself from Mia's clutches and looked at Ella. "Me?" she said as she wiped her eyes. "What can I do?"

"Can you tell us what time you heard screams from inside the house?"

"Must have been 9 o'clock," the woman sobbed. "No later. I go to bed at 10."

"What did you hear exactly?"

"Just a shout. I wasn't sure. I thought maybe Anderson had the TV up loud. He does that. Bit deaf in his old age."

"Does Anderson regularly have visitors over? Does he make noise often?"

"Oh no. Quiet as a mouse in there. Since his wife left him he doesn't do a whole lot. Got a routine carved in stone."

If he had a routine, the killer probably knew it thought Mia. "Do you know what his routine was?" Mia thought that if they could track Anderson's last movements, they might catch the unsub following him.

"Fishing on Friday mornings down Lake Carnegie. Grocery shopping on Saturday nights. The rest of the week he just tinkered around the house."

Not a whole lot to go on, but better than nothing.

"Did you see anyone around here last night? Anyone suspicious? Maybe someone you don't see regularly?"

"Not a soul," the old woman said. "And I keep my eyes peeled. If I hear a sound, you can bet I'm at the window right away. I didn't see a thing."

"But you called the police this morning?" asked Ella.

"Something didn't seem right to me. You see these trash cans out here? Today's collection day and you can be damn sure Anderson would have his out. You can set your watch to that man. When I got up and saw his trash hadn't been put out for collection, that's when I knew he was dead as a doornail," she cried. "Don't ask me how I knew, I just did."

"Do you know anyone who might want to hurt Anderson?" Mia asked. "Any enemies? Anyone from his past?"

The lady didn't hesitate. "No," she said. "Anderson never did wrong by anyone. Everyone who knew him loved him. Harmless as a dove."

Mia had nothing else to ask. She was running on fumes now, struggling to think of any questions that could possibly indicate why someone might want to hurt these people. She and Ella exchanged a look, both saying the same thing. They had absolutely no idea where to go from here.

"Thank you, miss," said Ella. "You've been a great help. If you need help with anything, please just call the NJPD."

The lady's finger moved between the agents. "You best catch this maniac now, you hear? Gut this son of a bitch like a Christmas goose."

"We'll do everything we can," Mia said, then ushered one of the nearby officers to escort the woman back home. Mia and Ella went back into the room, a slight bit of tension between them. Ella's face was as pale as she'd ever seen. The girl needed a sunbed in her life, or a vacation at the very least.

"What are we missing here, Ripley?" she asked.

"I don't know," Mia conceded. "It's like there's a barrier with a ton of possibilities on the other side, but I just can't climb over it. Everything's fuzzy, like a TV screen that hasn't been tuned properly. I can see a few images but nothing clear."

"Bear with me," Ella said. "I'm trying to put something together but I need a little more time to think. I can feel a string running through all of this; it's just hiding behind all of the bullshit."

"It's Tobias," Mia said. "He poisoned our thoughts. God damn I'd love to stamp on his skull." Mia slammed her hand against the wall, drawing the attention of some of the surrounding officers.

"Same," said Ella. "But we don't know what we're going to get from this scene. There could be fingerprints all over this place. There could be DNA on the body. If we look into Anderson's life, it might give us some leads to follow."

"You're a hopeful optimist sometimes, Dark. We got nothing from two public murders, and you think he's going to accidentally leave something behind at a scene like this? A scene where he had free reign and unlimited time?" Mia turned to the wall and saw a photograph of Anderson with his two kids, probably taken years ago judging by how young Anderson looked. "And the photo. The one that Floyd's wife gave us."

Ella's expression turned sour. "Shit. I didn't even think of that."

"Anderson's not in it, so that has nothing to do with all this. Another avenue we can't explore."

Ella checked the photo on her phone. She shook her head in defeat. "You're right. No sign of Anderson. Must have been a coincidence."

"Great. So we could be dealing with anybody. It probably isn't a former patient or a co-worker, so it could be any random lunatic who hates doctors. Not exactly slim pickings, is it?"

Ella put her hand on her partner's shoulder. "Ripley, if the roles were reversed, you'd be the first one to tell me to cool it. Getting pissed off isn't going to solve anything. You know this."

Mia leaned against the wall. A drink would be good about now. Or a cigar. Something to clear the mental fog. She prayed to God that Ella had something they could latch onto, because she just felt like she was spiraling further into the abyss with every new body. It was an alien sensation. The last time she felt so hopeless was 16 years ago when she chased a perpetrator dubbed the Executioner.

"I'm done here," Mia said, not sure if she was talking about the scene or her career. "Let's go. Maybe to the bar."

"It's 7:30," Ella said. "We don't need booze, we need to put our heads together. Let's hit the precinct and figure this whole thing out. I've got something in mind; I just need to fit the pieces together."

"You better have something, rookie. I'm relying on you here."

"Just bear with me. And I hate to say this, but the answer might have been right in front of us from the beginning."

CHAPTER EIGHTEEN

Ella paced up and down their office at the NJPD precinct. On the table between her and Mia, she'd laid out everything. The available crime scene photos, the personal photos she'd taken of Anderson Cooper's body, the court transcript from Connor Jansen's trial. Mia had two coffees in front of her.

"Two coffees?" Ella asked.

"Like I told you, self-regulation. Anyway, talk to me. Get all those thoughts out into the open. Now's the time to get crazy."

Ella went right back to the start. "Leslie was a care worker. James was a doctor. Anderson was a locum neurologist. They all worked at different places, but that doesn't mean their jobs didn't overlap."

"We already know Leslie and James knew each other, but I can't see anything that links Anderson to them. The only thing we can say for sure is that our unsub isn't looking for a certain *type*. These people aren't surrogates for someone else. The people themselves are the targets."

"Exactly. That's the main connection. Our killer knew all these people beforehand, so there must be something that links them together."

Mia rocked back in her chair and glanced at the ceiling. "We know this, Dark. Give me something new."

Ella started drawing on the whiteboard. She made three columns, one for each victim.

"I'm getting there. Now, in every case, our killer incorporated a medical tube into the crime. With Leslie, he just strangled her with it. With James, he stuffed it down his throat. With Anderson, he plunged it directly into his stomach. What's that tell us?"

"He's evolving. First it started as a ritual, then progressed to it actually becoming a component of the murder itself." Mia scratched her head. "Now that I think about it, this is insanely rare. Almost unheard of. A ritual that progressed to a signature was then incorporated into the *modus operandi* itself. Have you ever heard a case like that, ever?"

Ella took a moment to recall past cases. She visualized a list of serial killer names in alphabetical order and couldn't single any out. It would be like Richard Ramirez actually killing someone with a pentagram.

"Literally never. Now, what did Ethan Heroux tell us about Leslie and James?"

Mia checked her notes. "They both got attached to their patients. When their patients died, they took it personally."

Ella began scrawling in the first two columns. "No, that's what I thought too, that Leslie and James were just overly-emotional, but that's not what Heroux told us."

"No? What did he tell us?"

"He said Leslie and James struggled with recurrent anticipatory grief. That's not the same as just being overly-emotional. It means they both saw a lot of people die."

"They worked in hospitals, Dark. Of course they did."

Ella waved her hands around. "Not really. Doctors aren't around when people die. Their patients die at home or under nurse care."

"Maybe, but it's not a stretch to think that James saw plenty of death."

"I'm sure he did, but then we get to the tough part. These tubes. Obviously the tubes are a vital component of the crimes and they're indicators of the killer's rage. So think about it, where would a nurse, doctor and a neurologist see these kinds of tubes?"

Mia narrowed her eyes. Her expression became one of confusion. "Everywhere. Hospitals are packed with them. When we were at Princeton, I saw about a hundred of them alone."

"No, not the tubes themselves. Look at these pictures." She grabbed three crime scene photos, one of each victim. "Leslie, around the neck. James, down the throat. Anderson, in the stomach, or near the intestines. What does that remind you of?"

"Any surgical procedure. Anyone in a hospital bed. I was hoping you'd really have something here Dark but I'm not seeing it."

Ella rushed round to the other side of the table. "Ripley, look closely." She pointed at the Leslie Buddington photo of her dead in her car.

"Yes. I've seen it a hundred times. What am I looking at?"

"This tube is around her throat. It's symbolic, not literal. It's a *breathing tube*."

Mia bit her lip as curiosity spread over her face. "Oh shit. Why didn't I see that?" she shouted. "Of course. The tubes are symbolic. Next one. Grab the second victim's photos."

Ella did, holding up a close-up picture of James Floyd dead in the parking lot. A tube stuck out of his mouth. "See it now?" Ella asked.

Mia almost jumped out of her seat. "A feeding tube," she said.

"Exactly," said Ella. "And that just leaves us with one more." She pulled up a photo of the most recent victim, Anderson Cooper, sprawled on his staircase with a tube emerging from his abdomen.

"Tube in the stomach. Reminiscent of a central IV line."

Ella nodded. "Ripley, all of our victims dealt with end-of-life care. And what did our killer do to Leslie and James? He killed them, revived them, *kept them alive*. That wasn't him being sadistic, that was symbolic too."

Mia rubbed her face aggressively. There was new life in her. "You're a freaking genius. Why didn't we see this earlier? He resuscitated James over and over, keeping him alive. That's why we found morphine inside Leslie. He was mimicking end-of-life treatment."

"Bingo. It's all right there."

"Leslie dealt with people coming to the end of their lives. James would have dealt with terminally-ill people. Anderson...," Mia trailed off.

"Anderson's death is what pieced it together," Ella said. "As soon as I heard the word neurologist, it suddenly made sense."

"How? My medical knowledge doesn't extend very far."

"I'm not exactly an expert, but my aunt was on life support a few years ago. The neurologist was the person who made the final decision, if you know what I mean."

"Of course. The neurologist would look at the brain activity, see if it had deteriorated to the point they had to pull the plug."

"Something like that. And what did Heroux tell us? He said James dealt with a lot of end-of-life patients, Leslie worked in a care home where turnover was regular."

"Yeah, so what does that tell us? How can we use this?" Mia asked. "Are we dealing with someone who hates those measures? Someone against end-of-life care? Or someone advocating for it?"

"That's the next question, but there are a lot of routes we can go down here so I'm open to suggestions." Ella began to scrawl on the whiteboard while Mia paced around the room, just as Ella had ten minutes before. For the first time since they got here, she felt like she and Mia were on the same wavelength. Both focused, neither of them blinded by escaped serial killers. They had to keep this momentum up, otherwise it would be back to square one.

"We could look into all the terminal patients at Princeton," Mia said. "But a hospital that size? It could be a long list."

"Yeah, or we could see if Anderson Cooper had any involvement with Princeton in recent years."

Mia stopped pacing and pressed her forehead against the glass partition in their office. "We could try, but I've got a feeling that kind of stuff could take a long time to get. We're still waiting on some of Floyd's records to come through. Getting that kind of shit through the legal barriers can be a real ball ache. Take it from someone who worked the Donald Harvey case."

"That was 30 years ago," Ella said. "It might have gotten easier since then."

"No, it's harder if anything. A lot more hurdles to jump over. We'll keep it in mind, but there's got to be an easier way. We have to get this done quickly, and I'm sure you remember why."

Ella remembered very well. The sooner this was over, the sooner they could start hunting for the real source of their anguish. Ella didn't give the man any more thought. Right now, it was this case and nothing else.

"Come on Dark, dig into that encyclopedic head of yours. There must be something in there that suggests who this might be. What have we seen so far? What have we missed? Think back to the little things – that's where you excel."

Ella had already gone over everything more times than she could count. She'd replayed every conversation in her head so much that the words were starting to feel like familiar song lyrics. "I've done that. The only way is to find something, or someone, that connects these three people together."

"But what if it's not someone personally connected to them? What if it's someone who just has strong feelings about end-of-life care and chose these victims because they represented everything he hated?"

It was a possibility, but Ella was certain these were targeted attacks. "Ripley, you said it yourself. Why would he break into someone's home if he just wanted to kill any random doctor?"

"You can tell a neurologist just by looking at them?" Ripley asked. "He chose a nurse, doctor and neurologist because they're the ones who deal with terminal patients. But maybe didn't have to be a specific nurse, doctor or neurologist. Know what I mean?"

"Well, if that's the case, then any medical worker is a potential target. We'd literally have no chance of predicting his next move. The only way we could catch him is to rely on DNA evidence at the crime scenes, and something tells me this guy doesn't make a whole lot of mistakes."

Both agents went quiet while they ruminated on new events. Ella went back to her photographs and began looking through them, desperately hoping something would jump out to her. Nothing did, and so she checked her personal photos on her phone.

Just as she did, another message from Mark popped up. It was 8:30am so he would have just arrived at the FBI offices. She ignored it and continued to scour her photos. She scrolled through, finding pictures from each scene until she finally arrived at a picture of her and Mark together in a restaurant. She deleted it then threw her phone down.

"What about James's wife? Or what if you called that HR woman again? She might be able to give us some info about Anderson Cooper."

Her phone buzzed on the table again. Mia looked over. "Looks like Mark wants you."

"What a surprise," Ella said.

"Go and call him. Maybe it will give you time to think. It might do you good to talk to someone other than me for a while."

"No, it's fine. I'll call him later."

"I'm telling you Dark, you'd be surprised what taking a break can do. Just go outside, call him and get me another coffee on the way up. We've still got a lot of ground to cover here."

"Ripley, seriously, it's fine." Ella chose her words carefully. "He's probably driving anyway."

"Driving and texting? That's not the Mark I know."

You don't know him like I do, she thought. "I really don't want to distract myself right now. I'm in the zone and talking to him will just bring me out of it."

"Methinks the lady doth protest too much," Mia said.

Ella threw her glasses on the table and scrubbed the exhaustion from her face. Mia's comment repeated in her head to the point the words meant nothing.

Doth protest too much. Funny how language had evolved over the years.

But one of the words ignited a spark. Ella felt that tingle of familiarity.

"Ripley, what did you say?"

"It's from Hamlet. Shakespeare. Don't tell me you've never heard it before."

Ella thought back to James Floyd's crime scene outside Princeton Hospital. The blood, the deserted lot.

The car.

"You gotta be kidding me. How did I forget that?" Ella shouted.

"What? What did I say?" asked Mia.

"Nothing, it's just... you go and get the coffee, Ripley. I think I know a way of finding out exactly who our killer is."

CHAPTER NINETEEN

Nothing had changed. Tobias Campbell had nothing but time to kill.

Last night had been the first night in 16 years he hadn't slept in a three-by-six prison bed. Instead, he'd tracked down an old abandoned church that one of his associates recommended. He'd broken in through one of the smashed windows, made his way into the basement and slept among the mice and spiders. He didn't hear the sound of another soul all night, so Tobias added the place to his list of habitable locations.

He went back to Apollo House, the high-rise apartments sitting across from the river. There was still no sign of the girl. She hadn't been back here all night, which meant she was either staying at someone else's house or she was out in the field. If Tobias knew Miss Dark, and he believed he did, she wasn't the type for romance. She was out on a case, hunting down a symbol of her suppressed insecurities. Maybe once she caught this new killer, she'd finally be at peace with her old man's death.

Not likely, Tobias thought. Miss Dark would chase that dragon until death intervened, and that intervention would be a lot closer than she realized. In fact, as soon as she stepped foot back into her home, death would be waiting for her.

Tobias walked into the nearest town, hiding in plain sight. The smell of mold clung to his clothes after his night among the vermin, so he found a store in the town where he could change. It had been a long time since he'd done this, but old habits died hard, as they said. He entered the tiny shop, one of those independent shops with minimal security and begun browsing the jacket section. There was an old woman behind the counter, curiously eyeing him up and down.

"Can I help you?" she called out.

Tobias smiled his hollow grin and joined her at the counter. It was his first conversation with a human being since he'd left Maine, and for some reason, it was incredibly thrilling.

"You certainly can," he said. "I'm looking for a black jacket with a wool collar. Maybe sheepskin."

"A jacket like that in this weather? Summer's on the way, you know?"

Did this bitch want the sale or not? Didn't she know the customer was always right?

"I work with the scouts. It gets cold out in those woods at night."

"Wouldn't a blanket be better? Or some thick boots to hold the warmth?"

Tobias took a deep breath. If he hadn't have killed those guards in the elevator, he'd reach across the counter and rip this woman's spine out. Luckily, his bloodlust had not yet reached the point he couldn't control it.

"Maybe those too, but it's my collar where I feel the most cold. It's a personal thing."

"Well, I might have one," the old woman said. "There might be something hiding out in the stock room."

"It would be great if you could check. And while you're in there, could you look for a thick scarf too? Belt and bracers and all that." He had to throw in a convincer to avoid suspicion.

"Okay. Wait right here."

As soon as the woman was out of sight, Tobias got to work. He grabbed some rolled-up t-shirts off one of the tables, then some pants, and one of the jackets hanging up. He moved to the counter, grabbed a handful of gold jewelry, and he was out the door, down the street and into a public toilet in less than a minute. He got changed into his new outfit, pocketed the spare clothes and strutted out into the town. He continued on, far away until he was comfortably out of sight of anyone who might have witnessed his thievery.

He found a new row of shops, five in a row, hidden away in the backstreets. The one that caught his eye was a gambling shop.

Those old habits itched again.

He had hours to kill. He needed a source of amusement to pass the time.

Tobias entered the blue-tinted room, feeling like he'd walked into the future. He didn't recognize much, even the sports teams' names on the big screen up above. A group of old gentlemen stood around it with their betting slips in hand.

Sad, Tobias thought, but this wasn't the area he was looking for. He continued on until he found the slot machines and the card tables.

The area wasn't exactly busy, but Tobias was certain of one thing. Only the most hardcore gamblers would be in a betting store at nine in the morning. He picked up a betting slip and sat down at a table behind two gentlemen playing cards. He looked at his slip but kept his ears on their conversation.

"Two out of three," one of them said.

"No chance."

"Texas rules this time. You owe me that."

"Double or nothing?"

"You're on. Fifty each way."

"Are you kidding?"

"Take it or leave it."

He was right. Two old men playing cards with hundred dollar wages. He could use some of that. Tobias sneaked a peak at their cards. Bicycles. Red. Standard edition.

Easy pickings.

"Excuse me, gentlemen," Tobias said. The two oldies eyeballed him like he was from another planet. They probably weren't used to being interrupted.

"Yeah?"

"Instead of losing back and forth to each other, why don't you play a real game?"

The men didn't quite know how to react, judging by their expressions.

"What game?" one asked.

Tobias emptied his stolen jewelry on the table. "Look, I'm a bit desperate here. How about one game of Find the Lady? If I lose, you can have all this. Probably about $200 worth here."

The men inspected a necklace, a watch. Their suspicions grew even further.

"This real?" one asked.

"Looks it," said the other. "What's this about? It's not every day a man bets a stash of jewelry with a couple of strangers."

"I know, but like I said, I'm desperate here. My wife's kicked me out and I need money to get to Massachusetts. I got family out there."

"Buddy, this isn't a charity shop, you know? I'll play you, but don't expect me to go easy on you. If you lose, you lose."

"The very words I live by," Tobias said.

The man looked at his friend. "How about it? Find the Lady is a piece of piss."

"I don't trust this guy. He looks like he just got out the pen."

Tobias had to stop himself from smiling. "One game. No funny business. You can even pick the cards yourself."

One man whispered something to his friend. The other smiled. He searched through the deck, picking out three cards then passed them to Tobias.

"We'll wager fifty a piece," one man said.

Muscle memory immediately kicked in. He'd been practicing this routine for decades, but he couldn't remember the last time he'd done it in front of real people. For 16 years, he'd only had his horse figurines for company.

Find the Lady was the simplest game in the world. All the spectator had to do was find the Queen in a row of three cards. But of course, a little manipulation went a long way.

Tobias grouped the three cards together with the Queen on the bottom. He showed it to the gentlemen, then dropped all the cards face-down on a table. He moved them around a little to give the impression he was being fair.

"Find the lady."

One man pointed to the middle card. The other pointed to the one on the right.

"It's here," one of them said. "He did a bottom deal. I saw it a mile off."

The other man shook his head. "It was a fake deal you idiot," he said. "It's right here."

Tobias laughed. "Never mind, gentlemen." He turned over the remaining card to reveal the Queen. "Both wrong. I'll be taking my money now."

Tobias hadn't lost a step. He'd performed the trick a thousand times back in his carnival days and it was still effective thirty years later. If you anticipated the human mind, it left nothing to chance.

But as Tobias reached for the cash, one of the men grabbed his arm.

"One more try. Winner takes all."

Just as he anticipated, Tobias thought. "No thanks. I said one time only."

The man pulled out a roll of fifties. "Five hundred. What do you say?"

Tobias couldn't take his eyes off the money. He didn't need it to survive, but it would make things a lot easier.

"I have nothing to offer you in return except the clothes on my back."

"Deal."

Tobias looked around and saw a few people were watching their game. Suddenly, he worried that he might be acting a little too bold. What if someone recognized him? All this for a little money?

He discarded the thought. Even if the feds tracked him down, he'd be in another state as soon as his business here was done.

Tobias picked the same three cards up and arranged them in the order he needed. The Queen was on the bottom as always, but Tobias moved it to the top.

"See this? I'm making it easier," Tobias said. "The Queen is on the top."

The men stared a hole in the cards, not flinching or blinking or giving Tobias a moment to make the necessary move. He had a sudden impulse to drop the cards, grab them by their necks and twist them until they snapped. The incident played out in his mind's eye in stimulating detail, until one of the men's voices broke his trance.

"You dealing or what? Stop stalling."

Tobias thought on his feet. He adjusted the process. Instead of doing his usual deal, he did what magicians would call a top-change. It looked like he was placing the top card down, but really it was the middle one. A simple move, he just hoped that his spectators didn't catch it.

He spread the cards out. Both men chose the same cards again, but this time, the one who'd wagered the big money had picked the right one.

Tobias calmed himself. There was a way out of this. There always was.

"You sure?" he asked.

"Positive."

"Five-hundred is a lot to lose."

"So is all that gold."

"No it isn't. I lied. I just wanted to get in your head, make you think you had a chance of winning. See how easy it was?"

The man changed his selection. "Wrong," he said. "I was playing *you*. I just needed to see your reaction."

Tobias said no more. He lifted over the remaining card to reveal the Queen, scooped up the money and laughed. "You can keep the gold. It's worthless anyway."

"That's bullshit," one shouted. "You cheated. You lied." He stood up and came nose-to-nose with Tobias. "Give us our money back."

Then Tobias saw red. Rage surged through his veins. He had to use every ounce of willpower to not decimate the man right there and then.

"My friend, lying and cheating is all I know," he growled. "You don't want to question me, or I'll make a brain tumor seem like a birthday present."

Tobias took his winnings and made his way out of the shop. He needed to get out of here and quickly. He'd spent too long in the

108

limelight. He scurried out and fled to the nearest alleyway where he caught his breath.

There was just one problem.

He still suffered that burning rage. That unavoidable desire to kill.

"Hey," a voice shouted. Tobias saw a man in black, hood over his face. "You got anything?" he asked. He couldn't have been older than 18.

"No, I haven't."

Suddenly, the figure pulled a knife on him.

Tobias looked up and down the alleyway, completely deserted in both directions. Tobias showed no concern whatsoever. His heart rate didn't even speed up.

He'd never been so happy to be threatened in all his life.

CHAPTER TWENTY

"Make sense, Dark. What's on your mind?" Mia asked.

Ella searched the Internet. What she was looking for wouldn't be on any police database. Now that they had a solid theory, she knew exactly what to look for. The clue had been right there in front of her at the beginning; she just hadn't put two and two together. She thought back to the first crime scene she saw when she arrived in New Jersey. In the parking lot outside Princeton Hospital, she'd found something.

"Remember when I looked under James Floyd's car?"

"No?"

"I found that piece of wood. We thought the killer might have used it to sabotage James's vehicle."

"Ah yeah. I remember that. What about it?"

Ella scrolled through page after page. Lots of similar results, but not exactly what she needed.

"We're looking for someone who vocally opposes or supports end-of-life care, right?"

"Right," Mia said.

"What kind of people are the most vocal?"

"Is that a trick question?" Mia asked.

"Think about people who oppose causes. How do they usually go about it?"

Mia gritted her teeth. "They protest."

Ella slammed her hand on the table to punctuate the revelation. "Exactly. That piece of wood I found, it wasn't a weapon. It was a protest sign. I just need to find out what the protest was about."

She searched *Princeton Hospital protest, New Jersey hospital protests,* and a million variations thereof.

"That's a stretch, isn't it? Wouldn't somebody remember there being a protest?"

"Did we ask anyone?"

"Good point. I guess hospitals get a lot of them."

The words on the screen jumped at her like a ravenous predator. *DIVINE FOLLOWERS - PROTEST AGAINST LIFE SUPPORT – MAY 3RD – PRINCETON HOSPITAL, NJ.*

"Got it you son of a bitch. Look at this." Ella read aloud.

'The Divine Followers believe that only God has the ultimate word over life and death. Prolonging life is a punishable sin, and the Divine Followers will shout this from the high heavens until the end of days. In light of the recent laws, please join us on May 3rd for the biggest Divine Followers rally New Jersey has seen in years. We will congregate outside Princeton Hospital on Plainsboro Road at 12pm.'

"Religious lunatics," Mia said. "Great."

"Wait a minute," Ella said. "What laws are they talking about?"

"I don't know. Check it."

Ella did another search. *Life support laws New Jersey.* The first result told her everything she needed to know.

"Oh Christ, Ripley, look."

Mia bent down to read the screen. *"As of 2020, New Jersey's Medical Aid in Dying for the Terminally Ill Act goes into effect. New Jersey is the 8th jurisdiction to enact a death with dignity statute. The new law states that end-of-life care for terminally ill patients can be withdrawn upon reasonable request by those closest to them."*

"Does that mean what I think it means?" Ella asked.

"It means hospitals don't *have* to care for dying people if their families don't want them to. They have the right to die whenever they want."

"Shit, Ripley, could that be why this killer struck now?"

"It could be, but look into this protest group. You could be onto something here. I'm going to get that coffee I needed."

"Alright, I'll keep searching."

Ella dug as deep as she could into this Divine Followers organization. According to online sources, they were a New Jersey-based religious group that spread the word of God through protests, most of which ended up getting violent. Apparently their M.O. was to goad people into assaulting them so that they could sue for grievous bodily harm.

She quickly ran into a problem. She found pictures of the group's members, but no names. Apparently they did their best to keep their identities a secret to avoid legal consequences. Damn hypocrites, she thought. The Divine Followers no social media presence for the same reason, but she found a forum dedicated to their exploits.

Access denied. New users had to go through a rigorous signup process apparently. She didn't have time for that kind of nonsense.

It was a wall, but her whole job was to break them down. How could she get in?

Ella picked up her phone and scrolled through her contacts, ignoring more messages from her ex-boyfriend. She found a woman named Kathy Mansfield, one of the IT techs back at HQ and called her number.

"Hello? Ella?" the voice said after four rings.

"Hey, Kathy, I need a favor."

"I can try. What is it?"

"I need access to a classified forum. Can you get me in?"

"This is for an active case I hope?"

"Case W212, New Jersey."

"I'd love to get you in but I need a PWA form sent over. Can you do that?"

Ella didn't have time to fill in any paperwork. Lives were at stake. "Come on Kathy, please. I'll send it when I get back. You have my word."

"You've said that before."

"And I always keep my word!" Ella said.

"Alright, alright. Email me the link."

Ella opened up her email tab and sent across the URL. "Done."

"Give me a second. Just taking a look now." Kathy idly hummed while she worked her magic. "Right, I can get you a mirrored version of the members' area. The site will look a little ugly and you'll get some raw code in there too, but it's the best I can do right now."

"Will all the images be intact?"

"Yes. Link is coming across now. If you share it around I'll kill you."

"You're the best. You've saved my ass."

"Don't mention it."

Ella hung up and clicked the new email in her inbox. It took her to a blank white page full of black text. All of the site elements had been stripped away. It was tough to navigate but she quickly got the hang of it.

She scrolled through some of the threads, finding that the whole site was broken down by individual state. She located the New Jersey section.

NEW JERSEY FOLLOWERS – INTRODUCE YOURSELF.

DOCTOR ATTICUS APPRECIATION THREAD.

WHY JACK KEVORKIAN WAS THE REAL HERO.

She browsed them quickly to get a feel of things, quickly finding nothing of use. At the bottom of the NJ page she found a section called UPCOMING EVENTS. She clicked it. The most recent thread at the top of the pile said *MAY 3, PRINCETON, NEW JERSEY.* Inside, she found a 26-page thread documenting the protest in full detail. Again, no names, only usernames that didn't betray the protesters' true identities.

"Please, have pictures," Ella said to herself. "Come on." She scrolled to the most recent updates, posted this morning, and found exactly what she needed. Some of the users posted their personal snaps on the page. Some were taken before the protests began, most during.

There looked to be around fifteen protesters in total, not a whole lot. She guessed that the Divine Followers had branches all over the country, so they were probably spread quite thin. What she was looking for was a protest leader, someone who devoutly hated end-of-life care. In her experience, lots of religious believers followed these kinds of groups because it was a chance to feel like part of the collective. But their unsub genuinely opposed end-of-life measures, so if he was part of this group, he'd be at the forefront.

In each picture, one man seemed to be front-and-center every single time. A thin, wiry man in a red shirt and trousers. He was impressively groomed, with slick combed hair and tanned skin. He didn't look like a devoutly religious person in the slightest.

Ella ran out of the room, across the hallway. She peered her head into Chief Craven's office.

"Chief, could I borrow you a moment?"

He looked up from his desk, red bags under his eyes. He looked how she felt. "You got something?"

"Maybe. Maybe not."

Craven rose to his feet and crossed the hallway to Ella's office. "Try me," he said.

Ella pointed to the pictures on her screen. "See these people? Do you recognize any of them?"

Craven squinted as Ella scrolled through the images. "Who are these folks?"

"Protesters from outside Princeton Hospital on the day James Floyd was killed."

"Oh yeah. A few folks mentioned them but we thought nothing of it. Besides, they were gone by the early afternoon. Ain't no protestor gonna hang around until midnight."

Ella wasn't so sure. A vengeful protestor could absolutely do that, she thought.

"Hold your horses," Craven said. "Scroll back up a second."

Ella followed the instruction. She landed on a picture of the whole group mid-protest. Craven jammed his index finger against this screen.

"This guy right here. His face looks familiar."

The person in question was a plump man, huge beard, tiny glasses, dressed in a shabby brown t-shirt and cargo pants. "Him?"

"Yeah. I never forget a face, especially ugly ones. Wait here a second while I fetch something."

Craven disappeared into his office and returned a second later. He placed his laptop next to Ella's and began hammering away at his keyboard.

"If memory serves me rightly, and I'll be the first to say it ain't what it used to be, we questioned this guy once upon a time."

Ella liked the sound of this. Their unsub would almost certainly have a prior criminal history. Maybe not something severe, but he would have butted heads with the law at some point in his adult life. But then again, the Divine Followers had a history of causing trouble. Maybe that's where Craven knew him from.

"This your man?" Craven said. A police record spread across his laptop screen. A mugshot took up half of it. Ella couldn't believe what she was seeing. It was the same man, no doubt about it.

"God damn, that's him alright." Ella clocked his details. "Kenny Spencer. Thirty-two years old."

"Boy, this guy was a real pain in the ass," Craven said. "We dealt with him a couple of times actually. He's a general nuisance around town, but last year he got into a fight with a doctor."

"Princeton?" Ella asked.

"No, another one outside the city. I can't remember what it was about. Let me check." Craven scanned the record. "Oh, that was it. He was protesting outside the place, alone. Something to do with abortion laws. He confronted a doctor and they got into an altercation."

Mia returned with coffees in hand. "Woah, have I missed something? What are we looking at?"

"I got a hit," Ella said. "This protestor has a history of violence against doctors, and he was protesting outside Princeton the day James Floyd was killed."

"Damn, I only turned my back for a second and you've got it all figured out. Do we have a location for him?"

"No known address," Craven shook his head. "But he runs a charity according to his file. Gifts 4 God."

Ella searched the name online. The address came up right away. "Got him," she said.

"Good work, Dark. I hate dealing with religious nutjobs, so you're going to have to take the lead here."

Ella was already up and raring to go. "I wouldn't have it any other way. I'm ready to take this scumbag down."

It was incredible how things could change so quickly, how fast a person's attitude could adjust. They kept building the walls and Ella kept knocking them down. It was moments like this that gave her the drive she needed to actually make things happen.

And once this Kenny Spencer was put away, she could break down the bigger walls. Nothing could stop her now. It was all or nothing.

CHAPTER TWENTY ONE

Ella's heart pounded as they made their way towards the building. A field of gravestones gave way to a towering Gothic church, black as coal and impossibly ominous even by daylight. Ella walked up the pathway to the arched doorway; meanwhile Mia brushed past gravestones as she trampled across the grass. She rarely did show respect for the dead.

Ella turned the rusted old handle and pushed the door open. A heavy scent overcame her, but she couldn't place what it was. It was pretty much a general smell of *old.*

"I hate churches," Mia said.

"You might want to stay back," Ella said, "in case you burst into flames."

"Better to reign in hell and all that."

The interior was a striking contrast to the menacing shell outside. Gone was the Gothic architecture and inside was a fairly modern space decked with pews, an altar, and a gigantic chandelier hanging from the ceiling. Near the door was a small table with a handwritten sign that said *RECEPTION DESK.* Ella couldn't see another soul inside.

"This isn't like any church I've ever seen," Ella said.

"Have you seen many churches?" Mia asked. She hammered her fist on the table. "Hello? Anyone home?"

A side door swung open and a young woman appeared. Frizzy brown hair, massive glasses. She looked 21 going on 50.

"Yes, hello? Who are you?"

"We're the FBI. We're looking for someone named Kenny Spencer. Is he here?" Ella asked.

"Uhm…," the woman said. "What's this about?"

"FBI, and our business is none of your business. Is he here or not?" Mia asked.

"I'll have to check. I'm not sure."

Ella knew an incompetent worker when she saw one, and the young girl in front of her emitted all the tell-tale signs. She wasn't in the mood to have her patience tested. "You'll have to check? This place is emptier than a black hole."

The woman looked around nervously. "Wait here," she said and shuffled out of her chair. She walked into the middle of the church and stood completely still for a minute before disappearing into a side room.

"Talk about customer service," Mia said.

"Non-existent. Maybe we scared her."

"Hopefully."

They waited a minute, two minutes. Ella glanced at her phone, furiously swiping away another message from Mark. Every new message that came, she wanted to punch him that little bit more. God help him when she got back, because he was driving her to unhinged madness. Clearly the man had never felt the wrath of a scorned woman before.

"What's that bitch doing? Building a ladder to heaven?" Mia asked.

"She's taking her sweet time for sure," Ella said. "You don't think...?" She caught her partner's eye. Looked like Mia was thinking the same thing.

"Shit. She's tipping him off," Mia shouted. Both agents quick-footed towards the rear of the church in tandem. They followed the direction the woman went and found a small black door. Ella pulled on the handle to reveal a tiny office.

Inside was the frizzy-haired woman standing next to a stocky, bearded gentleman in a plain white t-shirt. Both looked like deer in the headlights. Before either agent could say a word, the man Ella assumed was Kenny Spencer was out the door, into the church, slamming the door behind them. The agents pursued, but when they got out into the main hall, the suspect had vanished.

"Where's he gone?" Mia shouted at the woman, now cowering in the corner.

"I don't know," she cried. "He could be anywhere."

"What *do* you know?" Mia screamed at her before running towards the door. "You search in here Dark. I'm going outside."

"Find this asshole's car. He can't get very far on foot," Ella called. She hurried down past the altar and found a couple of passageways, neither of which showed signs of recent entry. She picked one at random, ran down and found herself in a basement. She rummaged between a few boxes of old junk and found nothing but a few wooden crosses, most of them broken. She picked one up, realizing that the piece of wood in her hand was the same size and shape as the one from James Floyd's crime scene. This suspect suddenly looked even better.

Back up the passageway, she tried the next one. It seemed to never end, twisting around the width of the whole building. At the end of the line, she pushed open a door and found herself outside. Up ahead, she saw two figures positioned around an old green Honda. One hadn't seen the other. James was crouched behind the trunk while Mia surveyed the scene from the front.

"Ripley, he's on the other side of the car," Ella called. Mia rushed around the side of the vehicle, but a crouching Kenny shoulder-tackled her to the ground. Kenny fled across the graveyard, to the rear of the church. Ella was hot in pursuit, leaping over gravestones to catch up with the escaping suspect. The grass around here was thick and uncut, and some of the larger tombstones obscured her sight of the man. She stopped for a minute, gauging where exactly Kenny might have gone.

Ella moved between graves, shielding herself from view. The church was surrounded by a large brick wall with barbed wire crowns, so the chances of Kenny escaping over it, especially given his size, were small. She listened out for crunches in the grass but heard only chirping crickets and distant traffic.

In the far reaching area of the cemetery, Ella spotted a sinister visual. There was a dug-out grave; a rectangular hole six feet deep, the sides perfectly neat and trim. She waited too long staring at it, because several feet to its left, Kenny Spencer appeared from behind a grave boasting a giant, blind angel.

Ella covered the distance between her and the waiting grave in seconds, coming within grabbing distance of Kenny at the same time. He circled the empty hole, but Ella jumped over it and collided with the protestor. They rolled together on the floor, but Kenny pushed Ella off him. He might have been rotund, but he had some strength in those big arms. She launched back to her feet, straight back at Kenny and elbowed him square in the jaw. He toppled like a matchstick house in an earthquake, landing inches away from the empty grave.

To her shock, Kenny rose again in seconds. She grabbed him by his shirt and pulled his face to hers. "Don't you dare move," she said.

Kenny spat in her face, but what offended her more was his breath. She wiped it away with her sleeve.

"Kenny, I'm with the FBI, and little things like that can get you in trouble."

"And what?" Kenny screamed. "Let me go." He struggled in her grip, kicking at her ankles and lunging his forehead at her.

Did she have a choice? It was right there, begging her to do it, like an itch she needed to scratch.

118

"Kenny, if you do that again, something bad will happen to you." It was Mark's words to her, replayed in a different context. It must have been a subconscious thing.

"Try it you bitch and I'll sue you for everything you have."

For a man of God, Kenny certainly wasn't acting like it. Ella gripped him harder. "Kenny, I'm begging you. Please don't do this. I really don't want to do this."

"Eat shit," he shouted in her face.

She couldn't hold back any longer. It was calling out to her like a siren's song luring a sailor to disaster. She stepped forward, putting her weight on her front leg.

Then threw the suspect six feet under.

He bounced off the earthy walls and landed with a sickening thud. He lay motionless in an empty grave, and she wasn't sure that she hadn't killed him.

But she realized that she didn't rightly care.

***

"Dark? Why are you sitting next to a hole? Where's Kenny?"

Ella had to hand it to herself. It was a unique setting for an interrogation.

"About to get buried alive if he doesn't start talking."

Mia peered into the grave as she rubbed her shoulder. "Holy shit. Are you kidding me? Talk about surreal."

"Right?"

"Dare I ask how this came about?"

"Probably best not to." Ella looked at her captive, six feet below ground level. He'd risen to his feet, looking more like a zombie than Ella desired, but so far hadn't said anything. "Mr. Spencer, we can do this two ways. Either you come with us down to the precinct, or you stay in there. What's it gonna be?"

Kenny shouted something up. The acoustics of the grave actually made his voice a lot louder. "Blow me."

"Let me try," Mia said as she leaned into the hole. "Hey Kenny, you're on the hook for some pretty serious crimes, so I suggest you start talking to us. If you don't, we might as well just start shoveling the dirt in right now, because you're probably looking at the death penalty."

A long silence.

"Get me out of here," he called up.

119

"Why should we?"

"Because I haven't done anything wrong. What are you talking about, the death penalty?"

Mia nodded at Ella to take over. She looked down into the darkness, seeing fragments of Kenny Spencer but not his whole figure. Two glowing white eyes stared back at her.

"Mr. Spencer, why did you run when we broke into your office?"

"I got scared," he said. "I panicked." One of the downsides of this macabre setup was that Ella couldn't see the suspect's body language. That meant it would be harder to figure out if he was lying.

"Why did you panic? What have you done wrong?"

"You know why. Why else would you be here?"

"Just tell him," Mia said. "This is like trying to get blood out of a stone."

"Mr. Spencer, we have reason to believe that you have been involved with three recent murders. What do you have to say about that?"

Mia stepped back from the scene and made a phone call. Must have been backup to help get this poor son of a bitch out of the earth.

"Murders? I haven't murdered anybody."

Ella didn't buy it. Not one bit. "So tell us why you fled," said Ella.

"Fine. I confronted a doctor the other day. There. Happy?"

"Which doctor? And why?"

"I didn't know his name. Some guy outside the Penn Medicine Center. Okay? I got into a bit of a fight with him and I assumed he called the cops."

"A fight about what?" Ella kept the questions coming thick and fast. She had momentum and didn't want to lose it.

"Terminal cancer."

"Seems a funny thing to fight about."

"End-of-life treatment is a sin. It goes against God's will. Only He chooses when someone dies, not science, not doctors."

Mia came back and instantly resumed her wrath. "You're talking out of your ass. Science is the reason you're not lying in a pool of your own shit, dead at 30." She winked at Ella and whispered: "Might as well rile him up. A guy like this is gonna talk more when he's pissed."

"Whatever. Believe what you like. I've dealt with non-believers my whole life and you're little putdowns aren't gonna make me change my mind."

Ella let Kenny dwell in his grave while she considered where to take the interrogation, if it could be termed such a thing. She desperately believed this man to be the person responsible, maybe out of hope, maybe out of genuine conviction. Why else would he take the coward's way out when confronted, especially if he'd only committed a minor crime? Something didn't add up, and she decided to be vocal about it.

"Kenny, spare me the Jesus lectures because I don't care. Are you trying to tell me you ran away from the FBI because you got into a small fight?"

Kenny took his time. Ella heard him clawing at the walls. It must have been pretty terrifying down there. In a way, she felt bad for the guy.

"Yes."

"We're not buying it," Mia called. "No one does that."

"Mr. Spencer, you were protesting outside Princeton Hospital two days ago, correct?"

"Maybe."

"Don't lie to us. We've seen the photos. And we found one of your signs underneath the car of the victim."

Kenny took a long time to respond. "Can you get me out of here? I'm sorry I acted like a jerk, but I'll tell you the truth once I'm out. I don't feel right saying it while I'm in a grave."

Ella looked to Mia for confirmation. "Should we?" Ella whispered.

Mia looked like she really didn't want to free him. "As much as I'd rather leave him in there, professional courtesy takes precedence. Let's get his ass out."

"If you run, you're getting shot. Understood?"

"Understood," Kenny replied.

Ella lay on her stomach and reached her arms down into the depths. She wasn't sure why people used the term six feet under because this grave went much deeper. Kenny reached up and took her hand, the tension nearly ripping her arm out of the socket.

"Ripley, a little help," she called. "Heavy load."

Mia joined in, taking Kenny's other hand. They gracelessly pulled him out of the empty grave and back onto the grass. He scurried away from the hole, putting distance between him and his trauma.

"Okay, Kenny, explain yourself," said Ella.

Kenny clasped his hands into a prayer position and muttered something to himself. The agents repositioned themselves so that if Kenny tried to run, he wouldn't get very far.

"Here's the whole truth and nothing but," Kenny began. "Yeah, we protested outside Princeton the other afternoon. I hung around afterward. Long afterward. I strolled around that place until the early hours."

"Right, and why did we find one of your signs underneath a dead man's car?" Ella asked.

"I don't know how that got there. I swear on my life. But around midnight, I was hanging out in the staff parking lot. I won't lie, I was a bit drunk. Then I saw this man come out. Obviously a GP or a doctor or something. So I got in his face."

It was looking more suspicious by the word, Ella thought. This man was at the crime scene at the exact time of the murder interacting with the victim. His religious beliefs gave him a solid motive. Many judges would convict him on that alone. She kept a close proximity to him, ready to pounce if he tried anything shady.

"The guy blew me off," Kenny continued. "I just walked away, let him be. When I was about to leave the parking lot, I heard this sound from the other side. Like a commotion. I turned around, and there were two people fighting in the bushes."

Ella watched Kenny's micro signals. His feet were pointed towards her. He didn't create any psychological barriers. His mouth or lips didn't twitch. He maintained reasonable eye contact. By every metric, Kenny was telling the truth.

"What did you do?" Mia asked.

"I hid, and I watched it. I saw the one guy stab the other, then I freaked out and ran away. Yesterday, I heard about the murder on the news. I was the last person to see him alive. Obviously I knew someone would come for me."

Ella couldn't believe the nerve of this man. He witnessed a murder but his primary concern was with his own safety. People like this made her sick to her stomach. "Jesus Christ, you saw a man get killed and you just did nothing? Was that God's will too? Or are you just a coward?"

Kenny held up his palms. "Please don't. I was going to report it, but by the time I summoned the courage, the murder was all over the news.

"Sure," Mia said. "So, you were with our victim the night he died. Can you verify your whereabouts last night? And on April 30?"

"Last night?" Kenny asked with enlarged eyes. "Sure, I was at the church all night working, doing admin, printing flyers. I was here from about 5pm 'til midnight."

Ella collapsed against the grass. A sharp piece stuck in her neck but she welcomed the pain. Another dead end. The news sent her light-headed. "Can anyone confirm that?" she asked.

"Yeah, quite a few. Some of the staff here. Some regular customers. Loads of people saw me."

Mia didn't look happy about this new information either. "What about April 30?" she asked.

"Uh, what was that, Wednesday?" Kenny scratched his crusty beard. "I was down in Baltimore. Divine Follower rally. I didn't get back 'til Thursday afternoon. I got pictures of me there and everything."

Ella grabbed a clump of grass, yanking it out the ground as she rose to her feet. She hurled it in the empty grave, fighting the urge to not just jump right in there herself. This man fit the mold so perfectly it was like he'd been poured into it in liquid form, but they were chasing ghosts. Kenny had alibis.

"We'll be checking these alibis out, Mr. Spencer," Ella said, thinking that if she opposed it enough, maybe it wouldn't be true.

"Fine," Kenny said as he wiped some of the residual soil off his arms. "Can I go now?"

"No you can't," Mia said. "Local PD will be taking you in. We need to confirm your alibi and we need to check out some of the other protestors in your group. Even if you didn't do this, one of your friends might have."

Kenny composed himself a little, not anywhere near enough to undo the embarrassment of being thrown into a ten-foot hole. He spat on the ground.

"Fine, whatever, but if you want to find real murderers, you might want to take a look at some of these doctors. They're the ones who murder one patient while forcing another one to live in agony. What gives them the right to say when someone should die?"

Ella walked away, not acknowledging Kenny's spiel. Ripley called out to her but Ella continued on walking. The disappointment was fast becoming a heavy burden, and on top of everything else, failure was the word she couldn't scrub from her mind. Kenny carried on talking his nonsense, and she had to will herself to not push him back where he came from.

"Dark, wait," Mia called.

But she couldn't wait anymore.

CHAPTER TWENTY TWO

Ethan Heroux was simultaneously enraged and impressed by the FBI. They'd broken down his door and replaced it with a better and more expensive one the next day. He'd been wanting a new door for a while so their intrusion was a blessing in disguise.

The men from the installation company told Ethan his new door was good to go and that they'd leave two sets of keys on the side table. Just as they left, Ethan's newest client walked across his driveway. Ethan waited with the door ajar to greet the man, who looked to be in his mid-twenties or so. He was decently dressed, well-groomed, and armed with a pensive look that told him he had a lot on his mind. A good impression so far.

Ethan hadn't wanted to take on any more clients because his schedule was already packed, but this man's request had been something of an anomaly. The man had contacted him offering double Ethan's usual rate for one session, two at most. Ethan was more intrigued by the vagueness of his request more than anything else, because in his long career as a psychotherapist, he found that those individuals were the most fascinating of all. Bottle it up, let it all out in his office.

The stranger extended his hand. "I'm Mr. Davies," he said. "Good to meet you."

Ethan guessed it was an probably alias. Newcomers often used fake names until they were comfortable, but that just made this whole thing all the more intriguing. "Hi, call me Ethan. Please come on through."

The therapist led the way through the hallway into his office. His follower moved slowly, taking in the surrounding aesthetic. "Nice place," he said.

"It's enough for now," Ethan said. "Would you like a drink? Water? Tea? I'd offer you a latte but my wife's at work until late. I can't make them like she does."

"I'm okay thanks," Mr. Davies said. He looked around for a place to sit, idling like a lost puppy.

"Couch or chair, the choice is yours," said Ethan. The patient took the couch, just like they all did. It was a fascinating psychological quirk. In social situations, people usually chose the smallest seat in the room. But in here, they always chose the bigger one. Someone about the therapist-patient dynamic, Ethan thought.

He let the atmosphere settle. Therapy was a slow burn, and diving right in was a modern technique exclusively utilized by industry pseuds. If he wanted this man to open up, he had to light a spark under his feet and let it engulf over time.

"Tell me about yourself," Ethan said.

The patient lay down, something that movies and TV shows exhibited as normal but, in reality, was quite rare. Most of his clients just sat upright.

"My name's Gareth Davies, I'm 35. I work in a factory, the titanium industry. Not married, no kids, never been in a relationship."

"Tell me what's on your mind," Ethan said.

The patient took a deep breath. "I feel incredibly alone. I don't feel like I connect with anyone anymore. Do you know how that feels?"

"I think we can all relate to it on some level," Ethan said. "There isn't a single person out there, even the rich and the famous, who don't feel a little alone at times."

"But this is constant, and it's been this way for a year now."

"So, there was a time when you *didn't* feel this way?" asked Ethan.

"The only person who cared was my mom."

Ethan knew what was coming next, and in a way he expected a little more from this patient. Parental loss was a run-of-the-mill reason for mental struggles. Ethan really thought there'd be something more to it, especially for a man who seemed so presentable on the surface. "What happened to your mother?"

"Died. A long, agonizing death."

"I'm terribly sorry to hear that," Ethan said, settling back into his chair. The rhythm of the conversation was picking up and he could feel the patient becoming more comfortable, more honest. "Parental loss can be a traumatic experience. Do you think her passing is the sole reason you feel so lost?"

The patient lay perfectly still. "Are you?" he asked, words so soft he spoke them like a bedtime nursery rhyme. Ethan wasn't sure he heard him right.

"Am I?"

"Yes. *Are* you terribly sorry to hear it?"

Ah yes, Ethan had seen this approach before. Once the cadence of the meeting was set, some patients usually *tested* their therapist. It was a challenge, as if to say *tell me what you think you know.*

"Very much so. I lost both my parents in my twenties. It's a tough experience for anyone."

The patient sat up on the couch, something different about him. His wry smile had become a scowl. His fingers twitched in anticipation. Ethan hadn't seen these signs of anxiety when he arrived.

"Then why did you let it happen?

Ethan must have missed something because this man wasn't making sense. Mild schizophrenia, perhaps? Maybe borderline personality disorder? What was he talking about?

"Excuse me, I must have missed a step. Let what happen?"

"Those people. The doctor and the nurse. You saw them. You could have changed their minds."

Ethan didn't like this at all. The man's tone had gone from conversational to confrontational within a few seconds. The suppressed anger was evident in every word, every twitch of his fists. Something had stirred within him, and Ethan had to do something to quench it.

"Mr. Davies, I don't know who you mean. I work with several doctors and nurses. It's part of my job. And I don't offer advice in here, I just let people come to their own conclusions."

The patient slowly rose to his feet. "Ironic, isn't it? Letting people come to their own conclusions? Is that why she was on life support against her wishes? Against *my* wishes? I had to watch her suffer while they kept her alive. Is that what you'd call *coming to your own conclusions?*"

"Mr. Davies, I had nothing to do with your loved one's passing. I'm just a therapist. I don't work in the medical field."

"I did everything I could to make them see reason. Doctors, judges, legislators. I hounded them all right up until her dying breath. They did nothing."

Ethan pushed his chair away from the patient. The insurmountable dread hit him as soon as he realized exactly which doctor and nurse he was talking about.

The dead ones.

Fight, flee, or call for help. Ethan had a choice and no time to make it, because within seconds, the so-called patient was upon him.

CHAPTER TWENTY THREE

Ella stared at the whiteboard, spinning a marker pen between her fingers. Mia sat at her desk, a glazed expression across her face. The only sound in the room was the distant chatter from the other side of the walls.

It wasn't her turn to talk. So far, Ella had done all the work here. Maybe Mia needed to kick herself into gear and start producing something, because Ella was starting to get a little frustrated with her lack of investigative work. All she'd done was swoop in and stand by Ella's side like a mascot.

"Dark?" Ripley asked.

"What?" Ella didn't even turn around. She glanced at her phone. Another two messages from the ex-boyfriend.

You are unbelievable Ella.

I'm waiting...

She threw her phone on the floor and fantasized about stamping it to dust.

"Don't let things get you down. You did a great job finding Kenny, but things fizzle out. It happens"

"Don't I know it?" Ella said.

"So, where do we go from here? That's the next question."

Ella pursed her lips to stop her saying something she shouldn't. "I dunno."

"Come on. Think. Use that memory bank of yours."

Ella couldn't hold it back. It all bubbled to the surface and exploded in a violent tidal wave. Mark, Tobias, the case, Mia. She'd reached her limit.

"Why don't *you* do something? Like, uh, I don't know. Some detective work? Aren't you supposed to be the best in the FBI? Why am I doing everything here?"

Ella didn't turn around, but she felt Mia's wrath oncoming. The atmosphere instantly changed and the temperature rose by a degree.

"Come again? What's wrong with you, rookie? You're not yourself."

Ella slammed her hands on the table. "*Stop* calling me rookie. I'm not a rookie. I'm doing a hell of a lot more than you are right here. I solved my last case without you and I can do it again, okay? Stop with the condescending shit."

Mia slammed her laptop shut, walked over to Ella's side of the room and sat next to her. To Ella's shock, there was no wrath, no frustration, just calm.

"I'm sorry. Rookie is just a name that stuck. I didn't mean to insult you."

"Fine. Thanks."

"Now Dark, you might not believe it but I know you. I've watched you very closely for the past six months. Before that, I watched you around HQ. I know your baseline, I know your mannerisms, and they're all over the place. This isn't you. You haven't been you since you came to my house the other night, so you need to start talking."

Ella leaped out of her chair and moved away. "Or what? You'll ditch me again like you did last time?"

"No. I don't want that at all. But you know better than anyone, or at least I hope you do, that keeping secrets doesn't end well."

"You know what's bothering me," Ella said. "The same thing that's bothering you."

"I'm not concerned about Tobias. I haven't been since we got here. I've been focusing on this and only this. He might crop up for a second or two, but I put it to one side. I'll worry about him later."

Ella knew Mia was just playing the role. Mia was lying just as much as she was. "Quit it with the hard-ass detective bullshit, Mia. That's not true and you know it. Since you got here, you've been crippled with paranoia about Tobias. That's why you've been so distant. You even said it yourself."

Mia took a moment. She rubbed her forehead and kept her face concealed with her palm. "If that's what you think, then I don't know what to tell you. I've been nothing but honest with you. You could at least show me the same courtesy."

Ella refused to mention her troubles with Mark. She'd die before the words left her lips. She didn't want or need Mia's help with this. It was her own battle to win.

But Mia wasn't finished. "While we're on the subject, maybe it's time I make a few assumptions of my own?"

Ella peered at her phone lying on the floor. Since they'd been arguing, it had buzzed twice. Ella already knew who the sender was.

"Go ahead," she said.

"There's something going on in your relationship. Why won't you tell me what it is? You can talk to me about anything. It doesn't have to be work related."

Two choices. Reveal all while she had the chance, or keep it bottled up some more.

"Everything is fine," Ella said.

"Dark, they don't call me a human lie detector for nothing. It couldn't be more obvious that things *aren't* fine. And trust me when I say that if there's one person who knows how hard relationships are in this job, you're looking at her."

No. This wasn't Mia's problem to worry about. She held her ground. "If there was something going on with Mark, I'd tell you. He's a little much at times, but it's nothing I can't handle."

"Much? What do you mean?"

Ella grabbed her coat and headed for the door. The air in here was starting to suffocate her. "I'm going to clear my head," Ella said and walked out before she said something she'd regret.

***

Ella walked the streets, wishing she had a vice to comfort her. She had no such thing.

The worst part about all this was lives hung in the balance. Every breath she and Mia wasted arguing was time they could spend figuring this killer out. This unsub had a motive, just like every other serial killer in history. All she had to do was figure out what it was.

Pursuing Kenny Spencer with such certainty was a grave mistake in more ways than one, Ella thought. Kenny was simply someone who harbored deep religious beliefs and projected them onto the medical community. But the more she thought about it, the more they'd been correct from the start. This perpetrator knew these victims, probably interacted with them multiple times.

That left them with two options. It was either a patient or someone who worked with the victims. It couldn't be anyone else. No one would interact with these people so regularly than a patient or co-worker.

Her encyclopedic brain kicked into action, pulling up cases from history that walked the same lines as this unsub. There were hundreds of angels of death, or angels of mercy as they were sometimes known: medical officials who killed their patients. They were actually one of the rarest types of offender, and their motivations were not always clear, even to those who delved into their psyches. The prominent

129

theory was that angels of death enjoyed playing God, something that likely attracted them to the medical profession in the first place. This was true for most of the high-profile death angels, like Harold Shipman and Donald Harvey. These killers didn't want to hurt their victims; they just wanted to watch them die and relish in their dominance over life and death.

But there was also a subcategory of death angel who resented their patients and wanted to see their victims suffer in cruel and agonizing ways. There was also an even rarer category, the female angel of death, a lot of which targeted children and newborns.

Her unsub wasn't any of these things. If anything, her killer was the complete opposite of these things. He took the lives of those who saved lives. He was, by a very tenuous definition, an angel killer. Putting the link together hurt her head.

Ella stopped outside a doctor's surgical practice and watched a nurse wheel in a new load of supplies. She quickly moved on, not wanting to look suspicious.

There was one more type of medical killer, rarer than all of the rest. There had only been a few cases of such killers in known history. No official designation had been given to them due to their scarcity, but they were unofficially termed euthanasia killers or consensual killers.

These offenders willingly take lives upon request of the victims themselves, the most famous of which was Jack Kevorkian, the doctor who euthanized over 130 people in his medical career. There was the bizarre case of German cannibal Armin Meiwes, who devoured a depressed man he met on the Internet. There had also recently been a span of serial killings in Japan by the hands of a man named Takahiro Shiraishi. However, it later turned out that all of Shiraishi's victims had come to him willingly for what he called a *suicide experience.*

But her killer was none of these things, although he possibly shared some of the same beliefs. He believed that keeping someone alive beyond their years was a punishable crime so he ended the lives of those who did exactly that.

Ella thought back to Connor Jansen, the young boy who'd worked at the hospital alongside two of the victims. Of all their suspects so far, he'd fit the mold best. Maybe there was something else she could dig into there, not involving Connor himself but someone like him. A doctor who despised end-of-life care but had been forced to carry it out?

Then something sprung into her head.

Yes, there was someone exactly like that.

"God damn," she said to herself. "How did I overlook that?"
And she was on her feet, running back to the precinct.

CHAPTER TWENTY FOUR

Ella hurried into her office short of breath. She jumped into her chair and furiously tapped her keyboard to summon her laptop to life. Mia was nowhere to be found. Probably drowning herself in coffee like it was a booze substitute. Ella couldn't blame her; she did the same herself sometimes.

Her laptop screen lit up and she navigated back to the Divine Followers forum. She used the link the IT tech had sent her to get into the mirrored version of the website with all the private information.

She navigated to the New Jersey section then found the thread she'd idly skimmed earlier that day.

DOCTOR ATTICUS APPRECIATION THREAD.

It wasn't a name she was familiar with, but the pages and pages of information on this mysterious man quickly changed that. According to the forum post, Doctor Atticus was a New Jersey doctor who carried out euthanasia requests behind closed doors. He was a licensed physician by day and a murderer-for-hire by night, providing the people requesting his services were the same ones who wanted to die.

She read one of the articles that had been pasted into the page:

JUNE 2016. DISGRACED EUTHANASIA DOCTOR UNDER FIRE – MEDICAL LICENSE REVOKED.

62-year-old Flynn Atticus, occasionally referred to as 'Merciful Flynn,' was today removed from his position as a general physician at Clarke House Medical Hospital in Trenton, New Jersey.

The doctor, who was found guilty of euthanizing 7 of his assigned patients, was officially revoked of his license to practice medicine by the New Jersey Medical Committee on June 3, 2016.

Atticus reportedly removed multiple life-support measures at the request his patients or their close relatives, something opposed by New Jersey law. Atticus then falsified documents, claiming that the patients had died of natural causes.

The shamed doctor was sentenced to 120 hours of unpaid community work.

Ella read every word on the page about the disgraced doctor, feeling like she knew him well by time she reached the bottom. He was New Jersey's own Jack Kevorkian, and after his humiliating exit from the medical scene in 2016, she couldn't find any mentions of the man elsewhere. He dropped off the map.

Dead? Moved to another state?

Or maybe he'd begun plying his grisly trade in a different way?

Flynn Atticus was based in Trenton, around 20 miles away from Princeton. It wasn't impossible to think that Atticus might have been familiar with some of the doctors in Princeton who dealt with end-of-life patients.

The door swung open and Mia came back. She sat on the other side of the room but didn't say a word. Ella decided to take the high road. She owed it her partner after what she'd said about Tobias, even though it was all true.

"Ripley, I'm sorry. Again. I didn't mean what I said."

"Huh?" She looked up from her screen. "Oh, I was a million miles away."

Maybe she wasn't as upset as Ella thought. Thank God. "No sweat. Are you okay?"

"No, I'm not Dark, but that's alright. If I've been absent, I'm sorry. You're right too. I am scared of Tobias. He's my personal demon who's lived in my head for 20 years, and now he's coming for me."

"Well, when you put it like that," Ella said.

"But we're going to do everything we can to stop it. I'm going to fight until my last breath to protect both myself and you."

"Me too. You can trust me."

"I know Dark. I trust you too. But let's focus on this guy right now. One asshole at a time."

Ella glanced at her partner and saw the exhaustion on her face. Sometimes, it was hard to see Mia as anything but the diligent, hard-working machine her reputation awarded her. The man who'd mentally crippled her was hiding out in the shadows, and while Ella had the same worries, Mia's were probably twice as intense.

She wanted to give the woman a break. Maybe if Ella went out and back with a suspect in chains, that might relieve some of her partner's tension.

Or if she left Mia alone a while, she might come up with some of her own theories.

"I might run and get some dinner," Ella said. "I'm starting to get light-headed."

Mia jittered her fingers on her laptop then slapped the screen. "Damn thing is dead. Left my charger at the motel. I guess I'll come with you."

"No, it's alright. I'll bring you something back." She pointed to her charger. "Borrow mine."

"Thanks, partner."

"Back in a minute," Ella said, and slipped away.

She had no intention of getting dinner.

***

The drive was much longer than she expected. Almost 40 miles. The journey took her out into the New Jersey sticks, old stone houses and farms few and far between. Dusk had settled in and nightfall was only an hour away.

Finding Atticus's address had been easier than expected. According to the police database, he was alive and well, still living in his hometown. When she programmed his address in the GPS, she had doubts about driving so far.

Almost an hour of driving and she finally reached the home of the strange doctor. It was situated on a long, empty country road, without even a sidewalk to park her car. She found a small dirt patch just wide enough to fit.

Atticus's home was a traditional stone building, nestled away within a sea of trees and overgrown weeds. Dusty windows, Gothic roofs, and double wrought-iron gates that were invitingly ajar. Even from the outside, it looked like a serial killer's den. She had handcuffs in her back pocket, a taser in her front. She was still working on the license to carry a firearm, which they told her was coming *any day now.*

Ella slid up the long stone pathway, moving from shadow to shadow. The image that replayed in her head was that of her dragging Atticus into the interrogation room, presenting him with the facts and eliciting a confession out of him. Then, it was onto bigger things.

Arriving at the door, she felt enclosed by nature. Birds sang and bats fluttered in the trees up above, as though they were an omen of something more sinister to come. She took a deep breath and knocked on the old black door.

Shuffling on the other side. Someone was there. She had to remind herself that this man, if that was the person beyond the door, had killed people. He'd been in the presence of death multiple times, and such an experience changed a person. Six cases deep, Ella hadn't yet taken a life and she aimed to keep it that way.

At least, for as long as she could.

The door creaked open and a face appeared. Saggy skin, thin gray hair swept back, thin lips drier than a camel's back.

"Hello, sweetheart. Is everything okay?" the man smiled.

The pleasantry took her by surprise. "Hi, Mr. Atticus?"

"That's me alright. What do I owe this surprise?"

"My name's Agent Dark with the FBI. I need to talk with you about something."

The door swung open and Atticus appeared in full. He was wearing a brown sweater and loose pyjama trousers. "Well, why don't you come on in? You'll catch your death in this cold."

Ella gripped the taser through her trouser pocket. This man was just told the FBI were at his door and he was letting them in? Not even the least amount of suspicion? Something seemed off.

"Alright, but aren't you worried why the FBI are at your door?"

"Anything for a little company these days," he chuckled. "Come on. I was just making tea."

Ella followed Atticus inside, keeping a safe distance and a watchful eye. The interior was much like the outside, unkempt and neglected. Old Victorian furniture, a loud ticking grandfather clock taller than her, mahogany tables with swirly legs. She felt like she'd stepped through a portal into the 1920s.

"Lounge is that way," Atticus said. "Are you a no-sugar or a two-sugars type of girl?"

"I'm okay. No tea for me. I just want to talk."

"Of course. No one ever takes one sugar. Isn't that strange?"

Now that Atticus pointed it out, she realized he was right. It wasn't very often you met someone who only took one sugar.

She walked backwards into the lounge, not wanting to turn away from this man for a second. No one was this pleasant to complete strangers at their door. He was being overly-friendly, trying to lure her in. Once her guard was down, that's when he'd strike. He might be old, but if he was their killer, he was obviously a dangerous man.

The lounge featured more of the same. A torn sofa, a single rocking chair that looked like something out of an abandoned asylum. Atticus returned, two teas in hand. He placed one down on the brick fireplace and then sat in the rocking chair.

"Feel free to get comfortable," Atticus said.

"Protocol tells me to stand," Ella said, "but thanks for the offer." Now that he was sitting in front of her, the anxiety began to flare up. She wished she'd have told Mia about all this.

"Suit yourself miss. So what's the FBI doing at my door?"

135

"Mr. Atticus, do you…"

"Call me Flynn, please. I'm no more important than anyone else."

"Flynn, do you have any idea why law enforcement might suddenly come into your house?"

He held up his hands, like *you got me.* "Of course. I'm a disgraced killer," he laughed. "I'm always getting visits from the fuzz."

"Why is that?" Ella asked.

"Well, not so much anymore, but I used to. Any time something suspicious happens around here, they go straight to old Merciful Flynn's house. Sometimes I feel like a tourist attraction, just without the money," he laughed.

"A few years ago, you were involved in a high profile incident. Can you tell me about that?"

"Ask away. There's so much, I don't really know where to start," he smiled.

"Why did you do it?" she asked.

"Morality, my dear. We've all got our own codes of ethics. Do you think people should be able to die when they want to?" Atticus asked.

Ella found herself moving towards the torn gray sofa. This was a conversation topic she'd always wanted to get into but never really had the chance, especially with someone so close to the subject as the man in front of her.

"Yes I do. Dying shouldn't be a crime."

"We were born alive, isn't that punishment enough?" Atticus laughed.

She tried not to smile. She'd never heard the topic so thoroughly explained in so few words before. "That's good. You should use that one more often."

"Oh I do, dear. I said it to everyone who'd listen back when it all went down, but unfortunately no one wanted to hear it. Not the doctors, not the courts, not the families. To this day, everyone believes we have to prolong life beyond its natural course, and to me that's a damn tragedy."

Ella really didn't want to like this man because it would skew her perception of his guilt, but it was hard not to be drawn in. He felt like an old sage, dispensing wisdom from the corner of a seedy tavern. She didn't know what else to add since Atticus had smoothed the discussion so cleanly.

"I couldn't agree more. When you can't even die on your own terms, that's when you know things have gone too far."

Atticus raised his glass. "Hear hear! It's all about control with these powers-that-be. They want to control what we do, how we spend our money, how we live and how we die. All I wanted was to introduce a little freedom to people who needed it the most."

"How so?" Ella asked.

"Miss... Dark, was it? Sorry, memory going in my old age. Have you ever dealt with someone at the natural end of their life? It's heart wrenching, really. They're stuck in bed, prodded with needles, constantly tested, can't move. That's not life. That's a cage. All I did was provide my patients with the means to take action. I never killed anyone. I wasn't even there when they did it."

The emotions were overwhelming. With every new word, Ella felt less and less like Flynn Atticus was her unsub. He was too honest, too wholesome. Thankfully, the disappointment was anchored down by the pleasant experience of interacting with him. Maybe it was the subject of death giving her a sudden awareness of her own mortality, but the familiar sensation of disappointment stayed submerged.

"You weren't there?" Ella asked.

"Oh no. I supplied them extra pills was all. I told them that if they wanted to die, all they had to do was take them. All of that stuff about me turning off life support machines?" Atticus flung his hands up high. "Horse manure, all of it. I only dealt with terminal patients too. People who were going to die within the next week or so. The ones with no hopes of remission. But sadly, no one sees it my way."

Ella wanted to offer this man some sympathy but she wasn't sure how. She didn't want to give him well-wishes that his career might miraculously spark up again.

"Actually, a lot of people see it your way. There's a group called the Divine Followers and they think you're some kind of hero."

"Ha!" Atticus called as he rocked in his chair. "Those fools. I know them very well. Always coming round here giving me money for nothing. I've started asking them for holy water instead. I said it comes in cans in packs of six."

Ella laughed. Just when she thought she couldn't like the man any more than she already did. "Well, I guess they keep your mortgage paid if they give you money."

"Ah, I appreciate the gestures but it means very little to me. I'm doing alright in retirement. Still got my pension so it's not all bad. What bugs me about those followers is that they're not open to different opinions. I can see the other side of the argument, some of it makes a lot of sense. People who can't change their minds can't change anything."

Ella arrived at her conclusion. Flynn Atticus wasn't her man. Their killer was violent, motivated, mission-oriented. Atticus was a tolerant soul, just doing what he thought was best for other people. He didn't seem to have a malicious bone in his body.

Suddenly, the small lounge took on a deep shade of blue. Ella looked to the window and saw flashing lights behind the curtains.

"Lord, what's that?" Atticus asked as he slowly emerged from his chair.

"I don't know. Are you expecting visitors?"

"Around here? You must be kidding."

Then came the thunderous bangs. Ella's heart pounded like a bass drum. What the hell was going on? Atticus turned to her, his face enveloped by terror.

"Miss Dark? What is this?"

"Seriously, this is nothing to do with me."

Bang.

The old black door burst off its hinges and bodies piled into the lounge area. It all seemed very surreal, because Ella found herself staring at her partner. Behind her were three uniformed police officers, guns in hand.

"Mr. Atticus, hands where I can see them."

The old doctor stumbled back against his chair, throwing his hands up as he did. He looked too scared to say a word.

"Ripley? The hell is going on?" Ella shouted.

"Dark, are you alright?"

"Of course I'm alright. What are you doing here?"

Ripley threw Ella a pair of handcuffs. "Take him in."

Ella caught them and hung them on her finger. She glanced between the terrified doctor and the new arrivals, still unsure how this all came about.

"Ripley, I'm not cuffing him. He's innocent."

Mia kept her gun trained on Atticus, moved closer to them and took the handcuffs out of Ella's grip.

"No he isn't. This man is a murderer, and he's coming with us."

CHAPTER TWENTY FIVE

Ella leaned her forehead against the two-way glass and stared at the man inside. This didn't make sense to her.

She, Mia, and Chief Craven stood outside Interview Room B, one of two cramped and oppressive interrogation offices at the NJPD precinct. Inside sat a terrified Flynn Atticus, hands clasped together as though the man of science was praying for his life.

"Ripley, have I missed something here?" Ella said. "Atticus doesn't fit our profile at all. How did you find him, anyway?"

"I borrowed your laptop, like you said."

Ella thought back to their last conversation. She'd meant Ripley could borrow her charger, not her laptop. Miscommunication again.

"You looked at my stuff?"

"I saw that info about the doctor. It was just right there in front of me. I thought you wanted me to see it."

Ella put herself in Mia's shoes. She understood where she was coming from. A strange doctor, a missing partner. Ella would have pieced things together the same way and assumed her partner needed help.

"Right. I was just checking up on Atticus. I didn't truly think he was our unsub."

"Well, we do, because Craven found something pretty damning."

The chief jumped in. "Turns out this Atticus fellow was good friends with Anderson Cooper."

"So? Two doctors were friends. What does that prove?"

Mia held up the photograph James Floyd's wife had given them. "It doesn't stop there either. One of the officers spoke to some employees at the Tower Lodge Care Home. That little retreat they went on? It was a seminar about how to treat end-of-life patients. Guess who one of the speakers was?"

Ella looked at the suspect behind the glass, chained up like a circus animal. "Atticus," she said.

"Yeah. That connects him to every victim we have. He could have used the seminar to learn about these people, where they live, where they worked, everything. It fits, Dark. Don't deny it."

Ella denied nothing. She conceded that the connections were strange, but Atticus was a picture of integrity and morality. He wouldn't kill to prove his point.

"Did you ask him about the murders?" Mia said.

Ella clenched her teeth and shook her head. She hadn't.

"Well then. It's time we presented him with the evidence. Are you coming in?"

Ella led the way, in two minds about this whole thing. She thought of Harold Shipman, the murderous monster who played God with his victims, all while under the guise of a friendly neighborhood doctor. Angels of death hid in plain sight, posing as figures of virtue while addressing their sick urges from the shadows.

She opened the door and Atticus smiled, probably trying to disguise his crippling fear. "Please, agents, you know you have this all wrong don't you?"

"We'll ask the questions," Mia said, placing a pile of crime scene photos on the table.

Ella jumped in first. If this man had something to hide, she needed to address his betrayal. She'd felt a bond with him unlike any other person she'd interviewed. "Atticus, did you murder these people?"

She spread the crime scene photos out. Atticus eyed them with alarming suspicion.

"I did not do this," he said. "Why would I do this? I heard about the murders but I assure you, I had no involvement."

"Where were you on the nights of May 4, May 3, and April 30?" Mia asked.

"At home. Every night," he answered before the question had even left Mia's lips.

"You don't wanna think about it?" she asked.

"No. I'm at home every night. I've been watching a documentary about nine-eleven. Long series. That's kept me busy all week. If I'd have left the house any night, I'd remember."

That didn't bode well for him, Ella thought. "Atticus, you knew these victims, correct?"

"Knew them?" he asked. "No I did not."

Mia put the seminar photograph in front of him. "This ring any bells?"

Atticus glanced at it. "No?"

"This is a photograph taken at a recent seminar. A seminar you spoke at."

"Oh!" Atticus palmed his forehead. "You're absolutely right. I forgot about that. Yeah I spoke at that thing. It was more of a casual thing than a work commitment."

"What did you do there?" asked Ella.

"The new laws about terminal care were coming in, so they brought me in to explain a few things, mostly how to deal with the emotional fallout. That's all it was."

"Did anyone there oppose your beliefs?"

"No, they were all fine with the new laws."

"Atticus, we're going to cut to the chase," Ella said, "two people in this photograph are now dead. You were at this seminar when this photograph was taken. That means you had personal contact with the victims."

"Miss Dark, I assure you I don't remember anyone from that retreat. I was only present for a few hours then I left. I didn't talk directly with any of the people there. I was concerned how they might react to me, given my past."

Ella couldn't see through the fog. Was Atticus a truth-teller or a master liar? Both seemed like reasonable conclusions right now.

"And Anderson Cooper? You're friends with him, I'm told."

"I am. What about him?"

Mia tapped one of the photos on the table. "This is him, last night."

Atticus stared at the picture, wide-eyed and aghast. "No. You can't be serious. This is Anderson?"

"Yes it is."

Atticus forewent any subtle indicators of grief and went straight to crying. Ella glanced at her partner, no signs of concern on her face. It appeared as though Mia had reached her conclusion.

"That connects you to all of our victims," Mia said. "What do you have to say?"

Atticus wiped his eyes. "My old friend. I hadn't seen him in years. Why would I do this to someone I loved?"

Fair point, Ella thought, but psychopaths had their reasons.

"A falling out? Maybe you tried to convince them to see things your way? To end the suffering of those they were forced to care for?"

Atticus waved his hands around chaotically. "Miss Dark, I told you. People's beliefs aren't my concern. Plenty of people don't see things my way and that's fine."

"If Anderson was your friend, why hadn't you seen him in years?" asked Ella.

"How often do you really see your friends?" he asked her. "Check your address book and really think. You'd be surprised."

Another good point. Ella thought of her old friend Michelle and realized she hadn't seen her in about three years. "When did you see him last?"

"A long time ago. But I spoke to him on the phone just before he retired."

"What about?"

"He was struggling. One of his patients. He said it was the last straw for him."

Mia interrupted. "Sorry, but this isn't getting us anywhere. Atticus, if you don't have any solid alibis, I'm afraid it's not looking good for you. Dark, we need to talk outside."

Ella didn't want to leave Atticus alone, but she knew had to. There was only one way to clear his name and it wasn't through interrogation.

"Yes we do," she said.

***

"He's in your head, Dark," said Mia. "He's manipulated you into thinking he's innocent."

They stood outside the interview room again, Craven beside them.

"Why would he kill his friend? Why would he target people trying to learn about new euthanasia laws? He was at that seminar to help."

"We don't know that at all. Leslie and James could have opposed his ideas. They might have been against the new laws. Atticus might not have taken kindly to it. We already know that James and Leslie bonded with their patients on a personal level, so is it any surprise they might have taken offense to a guy who let his patients kill themselves?"

"I gotta agree," said Craven. "This fellow is looking real good to me. Victims, motive, criminal past. He's got it all."

"Two hours," Ella said, thinking back to their interrogation. "If I don't have an answer in two hours, then it's in your hands."

Mia scratched her head. "Two hours."

"Okay, but I need to talk to Atticus alone."

Ella knew that Atticus had information and she needed to extract it. However, there was a problem, and the only solution was to break the rules. If her years of reading interrogation manuals taught her anything, it was that sometimes you needed to give a little to get something back. Ella could light a spark under Atticus's memory bank, but doing so would expose him to confidential information.

But she saw no other way.

"Go ahead. We'll be watching," Craven said.

"No. Real alone. I don't want you watching or listening. I need him to feel comfortable."

"Dark, you know we can't do that. Solo interrogations are frowned upon. So are discreet interrogations. What if he confesses something that we don't catch?"

"You said you trusted me," Ella said.

"I do."

"So prove it."

Mia turned to Craven then back to her partner. "Alright. Alone. We won't listen in. You have my word."

Ella believed it. She went back into the interrogation room and sat opposite the terrified doctor.

"Atticus, it's just me and you. No one is watching us. I need you to be honest with me."

"I've been nothing but honest since you arrived at my door. I swear on my mother's eyes."

"Then you need to give me something. Something I can use to clear your name. You have no alibi. You have a connection to every victim. You have a shady past. You need to help me out here."

Atticus rattled the chains around his wrists. "Then tell me about your murderer. I may not be a detective, but I understand the human mind."

Exactly what she wanted. This was why Mia couldn't see the interrogation. Because if she knew Ella was giving out crucial information to a suspect, she'd be in big trouble.

"We're looking for someone who greatly opposes end-of-life care. He killed a nurse, a doctor and your old friend Anderson, a neurologist. In the first two murders, he prolonged his victims' lives by resuscitating them once they were on the verge of death."

"How did he do that? That's not easy to do."

"He strangled James Floyd over and over again. But his first victim Leslie Buddington, he used drugs to revive her. Injected them into her."

"Drugs? Which ones?"

Ella had written the information down back at the coroner's office, which meant it was in her memory bank for life. "Morphine, epinephrine, salt and sugar concentrate."

"Miss Dark, that is very specific. The average person wouldn't know how to do that. It also isn't something they could just learn from a textbook."

Ella felt like she was getting somewhere. "So how would he know? We assumed it was just a random combination of chemicals."

"Certainly not. It's very specific. But that's not what stands out."

"No?"

"That kind of combination would only be used to treat a very rare, very serious illness. An illness I've never seen in person, only through hushed whispers."

Ella pieced the fragments together. Their unsub had medical knowledge. Was her co-worker theory correct? Who else would possess the medical know-how to revive someone?

"What illness?"

"Fibrous dysplasia, more commonly known as Stoneman Syndrome. An extremely rare connective tissue disorder that gradually turns the muscles to bone. It's ultrarare, an alien phenomenon not yet understood by the medical community."

She'd never heard of the condition. "Why would these particular drugs be used?" Ella asked.

"Without getting too deep, that particular combination would greatly decrease joint tension, meaning the skeleton would become more flexible. Over time, Stoneman Syndrome turns the entire body rigid, literally transforming fleshy tissue into bone. The only relief is through chemical relaxation."

Ella suddenly knew where to look: any workers in the local area who'd dealt with patients suffering from this bizarre ailment. She clenched her fists in excitement and had to stop herself from leaping up right away. She still had more questions.

"And you don't know any instances of this illness? You've never seen it, or know any doctors who…"

"Wait," Atticus held up his palm. "I'm just trying to think. Like I said, memory is hazy in my old age."

Ella waited in anticipation. Atticus stared at the chains around his wrist and then shut his eyes tight.

"Oh, good Lord," he said. "Anderson Cooper."

"Anderson?" Ella called, her voice almost a shout. "What about Anderson?"

"I told you he called me, yes? Just before he retired?"

"You did. What was the conversation about?"

Atticus looked her dead in the eyes, like he was about to reveal the secrets of the universe. "Stoneman Syndrome."

"What about it exactly?" Ella said frantically. "What was he talking about?"

144

"He was the one who made the big decisions," Atticus said. "Anderson decided when it was time to let someone die."

"Right. And?" Ella was getting frustrated here. Lives were at stake.

"He'd made a choice the same day. And it really affected him. He wanted comfort from me that he'd done the right thing. He said something very specific, I remember thinking his choice of words were strange."

"What was it? Please, try as hard as you can."

Atticus went back into his hypnotic trance. "He said... *the boy begged me to do it.*"

"The boy?"

"I didn't ask what he meant. I assumed he was talking about another colleague. Some young kid who was struggling with the reality of it all."

Ella didn't need any more. She had everything she needed.

"Atticus, sit tight, because I'm going to get you out of here."

She darted towards the door and didn't look back.

Two hours to go.

CHAPTER TWENTY SIX

Ella sped towards Princeton Hospital, solo again. She couldn't do this over the phone. It was 9pm, and the HR woman she'd spoken to before wouldn't have access to her files at this time of night.

She abandoned her car outside the hospital doors, ran in and landed at the reception desk. The woman behind the glass jumped back in fright.

"I'm with the FBI," Ella said as she held up her badge. "I need access to your medical files immediately. Where can I find them?"

"Our files? Miss, they're confidential."

"People's lives are at stake. There's a serial killer on the loose and I believe he might have worked or still works here. Forget confidentiality. I just need a tiny piece of information."

Another woman appeared behind the desk. Brunette, elegant, professional. "Is everything okay here?" she asked "I'm the department manager."

The desk woman retreated, leaving the incident with someone on a higher pay scale.

"Hi, yes. I'm with the FBI. I'm looking for information about a patient. Can you help me?"

"Perhaps. Which patient?"

"I don't know."

"What department?"

"Same answer."

The manager looked around. She peered up and down the deserted hallway. "Come with me please."

Ella ran around to the other side of the desk and the woman led her into the back office. The manager shut the door.

"I saw you in here the other day," the woman said.

"You did?"

"Yes. You were asking about James Floyd."

"I was."

"Terrible what happened. I'm guessing your reason here relates to that."

"Yes it does. Can you help me? I just need you to search someone's medical records. Nothing else.

"I won't get in trouble?"

"This is all above board. You're not violating any privacy laws I assure you."

The manager turned to her computer on the desk. She typed in her credentials and logged on. "What do you need?"

"Stoneman Syndrome. I'm looking for any patients in the past year who suffered with that illness."

"Uh, Stoneman Syndrome?" she asked. "I can try, but that's a colloquial term." She typed away, clicked search and waited. Ella's legs trembled like leaves in a gale. She checked the time. An hour and thirty minutes to go before the others condemned Flynn Atticus.

"No results," the woman said. "I'm sorry."

"Dammit!" Ella shouted. She fell forward, almost curling herself into a ball. She thought back to what Atticus had told her. He'd given her another name for the illness, but she couldn't remember it. Or even pronounce it.

"Like I said, it's a casual term. It wouldn't be used in official records."

"Fibro...," she said. "Fibro displace."

"Dysplasia?" she asked.

"Yes!" Ella said.

"Dysplasia just means abnormal organ development. It would show up a lot."

"Fibrous dysplasia?" Ella asked.

The manager's fingers froze over the keyboard. "Fibrous dysplasia? Oh my God..."

"What? You know it?"

"Are you talking about the statue woman?"

"Who?"

The manager lowered her voice to a whisper. "About a year ago, we had a woman upstairs. They kept her in a private room, didn't even allow nurses or orderlies in there. Very strange situation."

Ella didn't have the time or energy for creepy stories. She needed facts.

"Why? What was so private about it?"

"No one really knows. But a few doctors caught a glimpse of the woman inside, and apparently she was like some kind of medical mystery. Her body had completely frozen, rock solid, like a statue. Constant pain, every day. The only people allowed to see her were her doctors and her son."

"Her son?"

"Oh yeah. I never saw the patient but I saw the son a lot. I caught him walking the hallways, talking to himself. A complete shell of a boy. Poor thing. I remember asking a few nurses to check on him."

Holy shit. That was it. The answer to all of this lay with this patient.

The manager searched the term and waited.

Tick tock.

"One result," the manager said. "I've never read this file. I'm not even allowed to look at it. If anyone finds out, I could be in big trouble."

"Can you print it for me?"

The woman nodded. "Just promise you won't show it to anyone."

"Promise. Does the file show which doctors were assigned to the patient?"

"Yes. On the last page. Every assigned member will have signed it."

On the other side of the room, a printer whirred to life. Ella jumped out of her seat and grabbed the mass of paper coming off. It reached the end and she grabbed the last page, turned it over.

Four signatures, their names printed beside them.

"Oh, f...," she said.

Four signatures, three of them written by people who were now dead.

Only one remained.

"Miss? Is everything okay?"

Ella was lost in her head. Everything she believed had been scattered to the wind, but then raked back together and arranged in a completely different composition.

"Yes. This is incredible. I have to go. Thank you for everything."

Ella was out the door, back into her car and on the road within seconds.

***

The man sat on the therapist's throne as though it was his own. The difficult part was done. All he had to do now was wait.

On the couch in front of him, the outstretched body of Ethan Heroux lay helpless. Tied, restrained, bleeding. He wasn't going to kill him, at least not yet, because doing so would be hypocritical. The therapist wasn't the target, he was merely collateral damage. But after three kills, he was starting to get a real taste for the macabre. It was as addictive as anything he'd ever indulged, more so than the drugs he'd steal off his mom's hospital table.

"Why are you doing this?" Ethan cried out. He was reaching the end of his tether now, the point where life ended and death began. It would be cruel to prolong the misery any more than natural biology intended.

"I already told you."

Ethan rolled on the couch, but the man jumped up to keep him in place. "I wouldn't do that if I were you. In your state, a sudden shock to your system could mean the end. Wouldn't that be a tragedy?"

"I can help you. You don't have to do this."

"But I do. You all need to pay for what you did to her."

"To who?" Ethan called. "I… don't….understand."

The man gave him another dose of the concoction, or the antidote as he called it. He'd studied his mother's condition to obsessive levels and found that this combination was perfect for jolting the body back to life in the throes of death. They'd used it on her, over and over again, to the point of inhumane savagery.

"My mother. You all played a part."

"I did nothing," Ethan spat.

"The nurse put the central line placement in her chest. The doctor put in her breathing tube. The neurologist denied her death time and time again, saying she was *too important to die*. They had to study her, this medical marvel. They'd never seen anyone quite like her before, so they locked her up like a museum exhibit. You make me sick, all of you."

"So why me?" Ethan cried again. "I'm not involved."

"No, you're not, but someone else in this house is."

Ethan squirmed against his restraints, slithering like a dying slug. Every move caused a sharp intake of breath.

"Don't you dare touch her."

But the man just laughed, as if the therapist could do anything to stop him.

"And there was one more person wasn't there? Your lovely wife. The nurse who comforted me when they finally took mom off life support, as though her forced affection did anything to undo the years of pain and suffering she went through."

"She did nothing. She tried to help," said Ethan.

"None of you helped. The doctor and the nurse told you everything about the statue woman. That's why they came to you. You knew full well what they were doing to her. They didn't like it, but they did it anyway. You could have stopped them, talked some sense into them. But did you?"

149

Ethan said nothing, panic and terror engulfing every inch. A beam of silver light danced across the room as a car pulled up outside the house.

The man smiled. It was time to finish his mission.

"Are you ready?" he asked. "This is going to be sweet."

CHAPTER TWENTY SEVEN

"Pick up the damn phone!" Ella screamed as she floored the gas pedal. She zoomed off into the night, retracing the path by memory. She'd already called the target ten times and there was no answer. Now, Ripley was giving her the same treatment.

Seven rings, eight rings.

Finally.

"Dark? Where are you?" Mia said down the line.

"Ripley, listen to me. You're going to think I'm crazy, but I know who our killer is."

"I'm listening."

Ella sped onto the freeway and throttled up to 90mph. Aldgate Court was around nine miles away. By her calculations, she could be there in five minutes.

"Atticus told me about this patient at Princeton Hospital. A woman who suffered from a rare illness called Stoneman Syndrome."

"Dark, let me stop you. Aren't you going a little wild here? You can't trust a thing Atticus says."

"This isn't one of my crazy theories Ripley; I've got solid evidence right here in front of me."

"Okay, go on," Mia shouted.

"I got the medical records for this woman. Her name was Angela Cheries. She had four people assigned to care for her while she was at Princeton. Do you want to guess who?"

"Our victims?"

"All of them. Leslie Buddington was her daily carer. James Floyd was her assigned practitioner. Anderson Cooper was her neurologist, and then there's one more person on the list."

"Who?"

"Clarissa Heroux. The therapist's wife. Remember what Ethan said to us? He said his wife was the one who referred James and Leslie to him. They were all involved with this woman."

Mia took a moment to respond. "Are you sure about this Dark? You're not clutching at straws just because you think Atticus isn't our man?"

"It's right here in black and white, Ripley. I got the records from the hospital. And that's not all. That weird chemical concoction our killer injected into Leslie? They're the same chemicals they injected into Angela to keep her alive. These medical records have it all."

"Right, you might have something there Dark, but who is this killer then? And what does he want with these people?"

Ella had only skimmed the medical report so she didn't have the full details. But when she put herself in a certain person's head, she could figure out why he was so hell bent on vengeance.

"Angela had a son. A boy named Jacob Cheries. Angela's condition basically put her in a vegetative state for a long time. Constant agony, kept alive way past her natural lifespan. Jacob had to watch his mom go through this hell, day in and day out."

"Right, but why now? When did this woman die?"

"Last year, but remember what we found about the new laws? This year, it became legal for family members to request their dying relatives come off life support. Our killer is furious at these medical staff, but he's also enraged that these new laws have come in *right after* he watched his mom go through all that suffering."

Ella came off the freeway and took the back roads by memory. Since she'd left the hospital, everything had passed by in a blur. It's like she'd jumped forward in time.

"Ripley? You need to talk because we could already be too late."

"Hold on. I'm thinking."

"I'm doing this with or without you, but I'd rather do it with you."

"Have you called Heroux?"

"Yes, but he's not answering. I've tried him about ten times. That's why I'm speeding to his house."

"Hold tight, I'm coming," Mia said.

***

Such a lovely home, it would be a shame to drench it in so much blood.

He picked up the therapist's ringing phone and turned it off, then he tied a tube around Ethan's mouth to keep him from screaming.

"You make a sound, she dies, understand?"

Ethan's eyes had turned blood red. He had the face of a man that knew death was imminent. A pity he only knew what that was like until recently. He went around the room, closing the curtains, ensuring no one could see in from the outside.

He left the therapist's office, shut the door and locked it from the outside. He adjusted the little sign on the door to say *SESSION IN PROGRESS*. That would give him ample time to execute his plan in full without having to worry about stray voices or cries interrupting him.

Just like the neurologist, he'd have time to clean up behind himself. He could remove all traces of him from the house and slip back into the shadows, leaving behind a perfect crime scene. Would anyone be able to connect the dots? What if someone uncovered that these four people were connected to the statue woman, as they called her? Could they trace it back to him, or would it be completely impossible?

Now that the mission was almost over, the thought of being caught didn't bother him in the slightest. If he went down in a ball of flames or spent his life behind bars, so be it. There wasn't much left out here for him anyway. As long as these people were dead, that was all that mattered.

Freedom was the alternative, and once tonight's events had concluded, he was going to disappear into the night. Maybe he'd go to Europe and give himself a new name, a new life, comfortable in the knowledge that his mother's suffering was avenged. Maybe he'd go to Mexico and put his murderous skills to use in one of the cartels. With talents like this, surely he had uses in a lot of seedy organizations.

Whatever happened, tonight was the night it all ended. It had been a year of misery followed by months of obsessive planning, stalking, learning these people's routines. The others were simple to catch, but Clarissa Heroux was the hurdle. Then the idea came to him when he learned of her husband: just pose as one of his patients.

He slipped up the staircase, found the spare room and hid inside. Downstairs, the front door opened.

His heart began to pound. He fantasized about what exactly he'd do to this bitch since he had free reign with this kill. There was no theatre here, only unbridled bloodshed. He could mutilate this woman any which way he wanted, something he'd been craving since he first killed the nurse.

Maybe he wouldn't even use the tube tonight. It could throw investigators off the scent. Leave it a mystery that people would obsess over for years to come. The possibilities were endless, all he had to do was choose the right moment to strike. She wasn't a strong woman from what he remembered, but she might be a screamer. The neurologist had been a screamer too, and that's why he'd fled the scene so quickly. He'd wanted to do a *lot* more to that old bastard but doing so was one risk too many.

Footsteps along the stairs now. She was on her way.

He gripped the handle of his butcher's knife and gently carved a line in the wall, imaging it was her supple flesh.

"Mom, this is for you," he said.

But then, something threw a wrench into the works. He pushed the knife harder, piercing the drywall.

"No, don't you dare ruin this."

There was someone else here.

That meant more people had to die.

So he needed a change of plan.

CHAPTER TWENTY EIGHT

Ella was the first one to arrive at 330 Aldgate Court. She jumped out of her car, darted to the entrance, and peered through the window into the lounge. Empty.

She surveyed the outside of the house. The whole downstairs was steeped in darkness, but there was a lone light on in an upstairs bedroom. She hammered on the door repeatedly, social courtesy be damned.

"Clarissa, Ethan, please open up."

Another car pulled up behind her. Ella didn't need to look to know who it was. She could tell by the revs.

"Dark, is anyone answering?"

"No."

Mia joined in the chorus of bangs. "FBI, please open your door," she called.

Nothing.

"Ever broke the same door twice?" Mia said.

"Ask me again in ten seconds." Ella stepped back, put her weight on her front leg.

Then stopped.

The door opened.

"You again?" the woman asked. It was Clarissa Heroux, still in her medical scrubs. "You ladies have a real problem with my door, don't you?"

Ella breathed a sigh of relief. They'd reached her before the killer. "Clarissa, please step outside."

"What? Why do you keep coming back here?"

"It's for your own safety. We believe someone is targeting you."

Clarissa glanced back into the home then walked out onto the path. She pulled her uniform tighter to protect from the harsh wind.

"Targeting me?" she asked.

Ripley pulled out her Glock. "I'm gonna head inside and secure it," said. "Dark, you stay here."

"Alright." She turned back to Clarissa, the only living person who worked on the statue woman patient. Ella had a million questions. "Clarissa, do you remember a patient of yours named Angela Cheries?"

Clarissa looked around as though she was hiding from paparazzi. "Miss, what are you talking about? Who's targeting me? Why are you asking me about Angela Cheries?"

"You remember her?" Ella asked.

"Of course. I wish I didn't."

"We believe someone is killing the people who cared for her. Leslie Buddington, James Floyd, Anderson Cooper, and now you."

"Anderson is dead too?" Clarissa cried. "Oh shit. Why would someone do this? What did we do wrong?"

"He holds you responsible for putting her through such torment."

"Oh my God. Well, we did. I hated every second of it. James and Leslie did too. Caring for her was the hardest thing I ever did."

"Why? What was so cruel about it?"

"The Medical Committee made us keep her alive because her condition was so rare. They studied her, long past the point she should have been left to die. Her life was constant torture. We did everything we could to soothe the pain. Anderson petitioned like hell to let her die but he got denied time and time again."

It made the whole thing even more tragic. The real criminals were the Medical Committee members. Leslie, James, Anderson, and Clarissa were just pawns in their game.

"Do you remember Angela's son?"

"Yes. Nice kid. I comforted him while his mom died."

"A nice kid?"

"At first. Once the committee denied his requests, that's when things took a turn. I mean, I can't exactly blame him. He was…," Clarissa paused, then stared at Ella, wide-eyed.

Ella stayed quiet, not wanting to state the obvious. The silence did the talking for her.

"Oh, you're not saying…?" Clarissa cried.

Ella just nodded.

Clarissa's body fell limp. It must have been a real emotion overload. Before Ella had to say any more, Ripley came back out of the door.

"Dark, it's empty in there, but I can't get into Ethan's office. It's locked. The sign says he's in session but I hammered the door to death. There's no one in there."

"Hang on," Clarissa said, "you don't know where Ethan is? I assumed you located him already? I only got home seconds before you arrived."

"No we haven't got to him. I called him but he didn't answer," said Ella.

"Ethan," Clarissa shouted as she ran back inside. The agents followed her to the office door.

"Dark, use that iron foot of yours."

She did, wasting no time. She stepped back, summoned up the strength, and booted the door in. Her foot went straight through, smashing one of the panels. Ella reached around, unlocked the door and flung it open.

"Ethan," Clarissa called. "Oh my God."

The therapist lay on his couch like so many of his clients had. But he was completely still, ropes around his hands, feet, and mouth, blood dripping from his stomach.

Clarissa screamed and ran towards the body. "No! Ethan, talk to me. Please." She slapped his face, checked his heart rate.

Ripley pulled out her phone and slammed it against her ear. "We need paramedics at 330 Aldgate Court immediately."

"He's alive," Clarissa called. "I'm going to keep you alive sweetie. Stay strong for me."

"Ripley," Ella called. "Remember the last crime scene? The doors were all locked."

"Yeah, but I searched this place top to bottom."

"He's here. He must be. He wouldn't have had a chance to leave."

Ripley pursed her lips, panic shooting across her face.

"Alright, you stay here with…"

"No," Ella said, putting her hand on Mia's shoulder. "You stay with Ethan. You have EMT experience; I don't. Let me find this guy."

"You don't have a gun," Mia said.

Ella let the silence do the talking. She still hadn't been cleared to use firearms in the field. She was only permitted to use them in extreme situations.

"I can't let you search this place alone. He could be hiding, ready to jump."

"You said you trusted me," Ella said.

"You know I do."

"So prove it. Keep Ethan alive. Let me do the rest."

Mia glanced between Ethan and Ella. She unhooked her Glock and placed it in Ella's hands.

"Only shoot if you have to."

Ella took it, nodded. "Stay with these two and keep your eye on the exits." She rushed out into the hallway, scouring the lounge, kitchen, and downstairs bathroom for any signs of life. She tore open cupboards,

157

lifted up ceiling panels. She checked the back door, locked from the inside. Ella removed the key from the lock and pocketed it.

Upstairs next. She sidestepped into the master bedroom, threw the light on and cleared every corner. She yanked open the closets, anticipating an oncoming attack.

None came. Nor did any from the adjacent bedrooms. The bathroom was a perfect square, every inch visible, none that secreted a vengeful psychopath.

Last was a tiny room, more like a closet, right at the end of the landing. Ella listened inside, hearing a tiny rattle. Or a scratching sound? She took a deep breath, prepared her stance and twisted the handle gently.

She stepped back and pointed her gun at the darkness. The pull-cord inside bathed the room in yellow light.

"Oh sh…," she began. Something inside caught her attention.

A red medical tube. The same ones found on every other victim.

The killer had been here.

Ella racked her brain, figuring out where the man could be. She thought back to her meeting with Ethan and hastily ran through their entire meeting in seconds.

Halfway through, she stopped.

I was renovating the basement, he'd said.

She pocketed the tube and ran back downstairs. There were no other entry points in the lounge or kitchen, but then she inspected the staircase.

"Ah-ha," she said. The door had been built into the wall, camouflaged. She fiddled with it, slid it open, then pointed her Glock down into the vast chamber.

A staircase led down into the blackness, but Ella pulled out her phone to use as a flashlight. She took one step, then another, barely seeing anything other than six feet in front of her. She could have called Ripley to help, but if this unsub had somehow evaded her, Ethan and Clarissa needed protection.

And something down here called out to her, like it was her mission and her mission alone to capture this maniac. Something to prove, maybe. Regain Mia's trust and look eye-to-eye with a man who'd killed the closest thing we had to saints.

Four steps down, she was able to glimpse snippets of the room in full. Piles of bricks, a half-constructed fireplace, the skeleton of a rec room.

It wasn't the image that hit her first, it was the scent.

Aftershave and blood.

Then it was the physical sensation of a hand around her leg.

The world moved in circles, rotating a sea of black shapes while her head and limbs bounced off solid wood.

Ella was on the floor at the foot of the stairs, her phone having fallen by the wayside and now illuminating a small section of the room. Something applied pressure to her throat. Increasing, mounting pressure to the point of broken bones. Ella tried to call out but the force made it impossible. She could only spit saliva and gurgle inhuman grunts.

By the small light, she saw a figure. A man with obscured features, reeking of aftershave and humming stale breath. His hands clasped her neck as he squeezed the life from her, but she kicked with every ounce of fury she had inside her. Her boot connected with the man's abdomen and sent him sprawling back into the darkness.

Ella struggled to her feet, anchored down by the sudden pain. She had limited vision and no voice, and in the disorder, couldn't tell which direction was which. She hurtled across the basement towards one of the walls, only now realizing that her pistol had fallen among the shadows. She frantically slapped the walls in search for a light switch. If her memory was on point, most basements this size had two switches: one at the entrance and another at the farthest point away.

Finally, she felt a pull cord.

The room shone brighter, illuminated by a single bulb from the ceiling. It cast an orange circle on the floor like a spotlight, and in that spotlight lay an object.

A butcher's knife.

Perhaps the same one used to subdue the man's victims. He must have dropped it during their altercation, she realized, so she leaped towards it since she herself was unarmed.

As she reached the blade, another hand appeared, both reaching for the same handle. Ella wasn't quick enough on the draw, and her assailant reached it before her. He swept it from the ground and struck out at her in one movement, ripping the wool on her top but not impacting flesh.

Ella retreated into the shadows, planning her next move. Her focal point was the man's wrist. Isolate the wrist, isolate the weapon. That was rule number one when dealing with an armed attacker.

He came at her first, thrusting his weapon chaotically. Ella tried to scream again but the pain was too much to bear. He'd incapacitated her vocal cords. Maybe Ripley would hear the commotion and come to her aid.

She found herself treading backward to avoid his blows, cornering and exposing herself a little bit more with every step. She waited for a moment of hesitation, right after one of his swings, then shouldered into his mid-section and maneuvered around the back of him. She tried to grip his wrist but the nimble man was too quick. He broke free of her grip, swung around and caught her thigh with his gleaming steel knife. The pain took her breath away, dissolving all energy and sending her to the ground.

The boy was on her, bringing the blade closer to her neck. She clutched his wrist again, keeping the knife millimeters away from her flesh.

But she was too weak now, rapidly losing blood from her leg. Her muscles weakened and her breathing rapidly increased. There was only so much she could take.

The man's breath on her face reminded her of her battle with Kenny Spencer the day before. She took a page out of his book, maybe a perverse version of the Bible, and spat a load of phlegm into her attacker's face. It dripped off, landing on her own wrist. It wasn't a martial arts move and it wouldn't be permitted in a boxing ring, but it distracted the man long enough for Ella to make her escape.

The boy shook his head to remove the spit, and that's when Ella was able to lift up her knee into his groin. With one leg wrapped around him, she projected all of her bodyweight to one side and rolled on top of the man. She rammed one knee deeper into his groin; the most amateur castration one could perform without surgical tools.

He grunted deeply, not screaming, possibly because he knew it would draw unwanted attention. In the few seconds she had the advantage, her priority became the weapon. Ella pinned the wielding arm down and shoved her elbow into his wrist. His bones cracked, unhooking his fingers and freeing the weapon from his grip. She pushed it away into the shadows, far out of reach. Now it was a fair fight.

But the boy had come prepared.

Something else took her breath away. Another puncture, to her side this time. The air left her body in one violent gust and she collapsed beside the man. He removed a penknife from her flesh, now completely drenched in her blood.

She'd been stabbed before, even shot. But the searing pain from the man's attack was unlike any pain she'd felt in her life. It felt like she'd swallowed a hundred scorpions, all of which were taking their frustrations out on her internal organs. Her breathing became erratic and one side of her body fell completely numb. There was no feeling in her right arm or leg.

Ella fell onto her back, at the attacker's mercy. She tried to shake the paralysis away, trying to create a ripple effect from her left to her right. He mounted her, the penknife against her throat again.

"Shhh," he whispered. "You shouldn't have come here."

The son of the statue woman. She'd never seen him before, or even pictures of him, but she'd seen pictures of Angela Cheries. He raised his weapon high.

"You look just like your mom," she said, each word an agonizing, foul grunt.

He stopped.

Now was her chance. Not to kill, but to stall.

"I have her file. From the hospital. I can give it you," she choked. Every word felt like she was swallowing a razorblade.

"Lies," he said, quietly.

"They did what they could." She had to pause between words. "Those docs. They loved her. Like you do."

"No. They made her suffer," he said, louder this time.

Ella lay back and accepted that she may die here, suddenly feeling more sympathy for Angela Cheries than she had before. All she needed was Ripley's attention, then Jacob Cheries certainly wasn't getting out of here alive. If she was distracted, there was a chance he could slip out of the house without Ripley noticing.

"How would she feel...," Ella stopped again. "Knowing that her son..."

Her own blood dripped from the knife onto her lips. Feeling returned to her fingertips, slowly crept up her arm. She gripped her thigh, still bleeding, and felt something in her pocket.

The thing that could save her.

"Knowing that her son what?"

"Knowing her son... grew up to be...," she uttered.

She felt new life in her limbs, and with her renewed vigor, she prepared for one final maneuver.

"Grew up to be what?"

"A loser."

Jacob Cheries screamed something unintelligible, gripped his weapon with fury.

But Ella threw him off with one colossal thrust, sending him face down to the concrete. She staggered to her feet, pulled out the object in her pocket and fell on his back.

It all happened in the blink of an eye, and in her weakened state, she wasn't sure how much of it was real. But when she saw the medical tube in her hand, reality came coursing back.

Ella tightened the tube around Jacob's neck, choking the life from him, straining his neck muscles to near obliteration. Jacob gripped his neck to relieve tension but failed. He spat and cried, but Ella didn't release the grip, thinking of the victims, their families, Atticus. This was for them. Doctors weren't the lords of life and death. She was. She could choose whether or not this son of a bitch lived or died right here on this basement floor.

Jacob's face turned blue, lifeless.

His body went limp.

A sign of impending demise.

The lord of life and death.

Suddenly, she wasn't in a basement anymore. She was in a nondescript room, and the neck she was crushing belonged to someone else. Tobias Campbell coughed and spluttered while the life vanished from his face. In his dying moments, he smiled.

But it wasn't Ella's choice to make.

She was back in the basement.

She chose life.

Her grip loosened, dropping the medical tube to the floor.

"Dark!" a voice shouted as she collapsed off the man into her own heap. The concrete did nothing to cushion her fall, flaring up her stab wounds as she hit. Blood had flowed from two gaping holes in her body, and their battle had created a single-tone abstract painting on the ground. Her eyes closed, not of her own doing.

"Ella, talk to me, dammit," Ripley shouted, slapping her face over and over. "Come on you bitch. Don't you fucking die on me."

She thought of everything she had to live for. Turns out it wasn't much, but there was unfinished business to attend to. They said people who died with unfinished business came back as vengeful ghosts, haunting the same area they died in for the rest of time.

She didn't want to spend eternity in a basement.

"Ella, God dammit woman, it's just blood. Come back to me."

She didn't believe in the afterlife anyway, but it was motivation enough.

Ella opened her eyes and saw her partner, crying. It didn't look right, this hard-ass woman showing such emotion.

"Dark! Stay with me. Paramedics are upstairs. They'll be down any second."

Ella just laughed.

"One down, one to go," said the lord of life and death.

Again, she chose life.

CHAPTER TWENTY NINE

Ella sat in Ethan Heroux's front garden with a thick towel wrapped around her. She wasn't sure why, but paramedics always seemed to wrap people in towels. Although, if this case taught her anything, it was that her medical knowledge wasn't always the best.

Two ambulances and three police cars sat in the driveway. A group of officers escorted the shackled Jacob Cheries into the back of one of the ambulances. He was a bloody mess, most of it hers. Before they shut the door, he locked eyes with the woman who'd apprehended him, and nearly killed him.

Tonight, he was the luckiest person of all of them.

"A few more seconds and you'd have killed him," said Mia. She took a seat beside her partner on the fancy bench. "That's what the medic said, anyway."

"Shame," Ella said, her voicebox still shattered but healed enough to communicate.

"You did the right thing, letting him go."

"I know. But when I saw those poor victims in my head, I just wanted to snap his neck clean. But just as I was on the cusp, I let him go. I had to. I couldn't go through with it."

Again, Ella imagined Tobias Campbell in the suspect's place. If it really was him, could she go through with it? Knowingly end his life by her hand?

Now that she'd been in the exact predicament, lived it, the truth was she wouldn't know if she could go through with it until she was in the moment. If someone asked her right now, the answer would be no. But if she could see his face, feel his presence, see that sickly grin.

She didn't know.

"Oh yeah, been there," Mia said. "That guy is going to prison for the rest of his life. Trust me, that's a lot worse than death."

"The paramedics arrived while you were downstairs. That's why it took so long to hear the banging."

"Yeah, I guessed. Bad timing. Shit happens."

"But you know what? You were right. You did all this. You solved this one, pretty much without me. If it wasn't for you, poor Atticus would be in a cell right now."

"You let him go, right?" Ella asked.

"Made the call ten minutes ago."

"How's Ethan?"

"Alive. His stab wounds were minor. Jacob just subdued him, probably planned on killing him once he was done with Clarissa. Ethan said Jacob posed as a patient to get inside their house."

"Smart," Ella said. She suddenly felt like she was in the right place, at the right time. Like she was meant to be here. This was fate doing its work, if such a thing existed. In this wonderful garden beneath the stars, she felt like she could say anything.

"Ripley, Mark hit me."

Mia raised her eyebrows. "Seriously?"

"Seriously. A few days ago. He slapped me."

"Fuck. Were you arguing or something?"

"No. You might not like hearing this, but Mark's an abuser. A harasser. He doesn't leave me alone, ever. On my last case, he accused me of sleeping with Byford. This case, he's text me 50 times in two days. He says I can't leave him."

Ella expected wrath on Mia's part. She expected fury, threatening Mark's life.

She wasn't sure if this response was better or worse.

"Well. Poor Mark, that's all I'm gonna say."

"Huh?" Ella wasn't sure she heard it right. "Poor Mark?"

"How many serial killers you took down? Five?"

"Six."

"You just took down a guy with two knives in a basement so dark I couldn't even see my hands. Remember down in California? You wrestled a serial killer with a shotgun and came out on top. Remember when we went to that art show in Seattle, and you battered that seven-foot muscle freak?"

"Good times, huh?"

"Yeah, but my point is that birds shouldn't pick fights with lions. Mark is messing with the wrong agent. I'm sorry, I had no idea he was like that."

"I guess people like that hide it well."

"So, what are you going to do about it?" Mia asked.

"What do you think I should do?"

"It's not my choice. Do you want him in your life?"

"No."

"There's your answer."

A surprising reaction, Ella thought. She expected a lot worse. She was glad she put things in simple terms too. The last thing she wanted right now was a lecture. Mark had to go, one way or another.

"Thanks for saving my life," Ella said.

Mia put her hand on Ella's knee. It stung a little, but Ella didn't show it.

"Thanks for proving me wrong. It's good to have a partner who takes the initiative. And doesn't blow up gas stations."

"We could always swing by one on the way home."

"Alright. As long as it's a small one." Mia stood up, took Ella's hand and helped her to her feet. "But first, you need to sit with the medics. You've lost a lot of blood."

"'Tis but a scratch."

"Yeah yeah. Let's go." Mia held her arm out as a barrier. "One more thing before we go, Dark."

"What's that?"

Mia leaned in and whispered, "You tell anyone you saw me crying and you're dead."

Ella laughed, her first real laugh in a long time.

So much for secrets, she thought.

* * *

Ella took a taxi from Reagan International Airport to her apartment, as driving was apparently out of the question. It was the early hours of the morning by the time she got home, and all she wanted to do was sleep off the exhaustion. The way she felt, she probably wouldn't wake up until next weekend. Luckily, Edis said he didn't want to see her in the office for at least two weeks. He called it a perk of the job, but such a description felt bittersweet.

The taxi dropped her outside her apartment gates. Ella shuffled out of the car, still woozy from her stab wounds but steady on her feet nonetheless. She pushed in the pin code then had to shoulder the gates to get them open. There wasn't enough strength left in her biceps to do the job.

She hobbled to the door, dreading the process of finding her keys in her bag. But as she eyeballed the doorway to her apartment complex, she saw a silhouetted figure against the glass panels.

Recent events had all but numbed her paranoia, but it all came surging back in one violent tsunami, crashing against her skull and muddling her thoughts.

166

Was it him?

It couldn't be.

The figure edged closer to her.

Not now. Of all the times it could happen, not now.

"I really didn't want it to come to this," the figure said.

That familiar voice, the voice she heard whenever she doubted herself. It was right in front of her, begging her to take action.

Not Tobias, but Mark Balzano.

"Mark, leave me alone."

"I've been texting and calling for two days. Mind telling me why you haven't replied?"

"Busy."

"Too busy to check in?"

"Yup."

"Bullshit. You've been hiding," Mark shouted. He moved closer to her, blocking off her path.

"I've got nothing to hide."

"What have you been doing? Who have you been with?"

Ella shrugged. "A few people."

"Like who?"

"Couple of doctors. None of your business."

"You're really testing me here, Ella. I don't take kindly to that, understand? You need to start being straight with me or things could get real ugly around here."

In this new light, after coming face-to-face with death, Ella realized that this man didn't scare her in the slightest anymore. He was a poor soul plagued with insecurities, insecurities that weren't hers to address. He could threaten her, he could fight her, but she wasn't going to give in to his ridiculous demands.

Ella rummaged for her keys in her bag. "Sure they will. You gonna let me past now?"

"Not until you tell me what I need to know."

"What's that?"

"That you're ready to take me back. That you're ready to start again."

Ella tutted. "Oh dear, what gave you that idea?"

He moved closer still, close enough to feel his breath on her face. He had that familiar scent, the one she once associated with animal attraction but now made her wretch.

"Well, if you've been reading my messages, you'd know."

"Uh oh. Well, I haven't read shit. In fact, I think I blocked your number."

Mark paced the width of the pathway. Ella had seen this before. She knew what was coming, and on this day, she welcomed it.

"Are you *kidding* me?" he shouted, probably waking up some of the neighbors in the process. It was fine, the more people who witnessed this, the better. Hell, the whole block could watch it if they wanted. Prying eyes perched at every window up to the skies, like a modern day Colosseum. All thirsty to watch the lion devour the prey.

"Nope. I'm not kidding."

"Have you met someone else? Is that why you're being such a bitch?"

"Yeah, maybe. Now you gonna move or what? I'd love to talk but I got stuff to do."

Mark's face burnt red. He sniffed his nose repeatedly like he always did when he got flustered. She first saw it at the restaurant when he'd screamed at a patron for no reason.

"You're not taking this seriously, are you?"

"Nope."

Mark pushed his forehead against hers. "Ella, you're making this very hard for me. What do I have to do to get you to see *sense?*" He clutched his fist and raised it high, threateningly. If he was going to hit her, he'd be a lot faster.

The intense pain was still very much present, but adrenaline had momentarily soothed it. The old Ella was lying dormant inside her, the pre-injury Ella. The martial artist that could punch holes in brick walls. The marksman that could snipe a target from a hundred yards away. All she needed was an excuse to wake her up.

"You can't do anything. You gotta quench that heat, or it's gonna burn you up, okay buddy?"

The colloquialism overwhelmed her ex-boyfriend. She spotted the signs a mile away. It was almost too easy. Mark's shoulder jolted backward, the sure-fire sign that he was about to throw a punch. Ella saw it in slow motion: the tensed shoulder, the rising arm, the subtle step backward.

But she beat him to it.

Ella clenched her fist into a ball of white fury, stepped forward and launched it directly at Mark's nose.

At the moment of impact, it felt like the world had lifted off her shoulders. All of the tension exploded in a blast of fleshy tissue and blood and bone. Mark unceremoniously toppled back into the bushes, clutching his nose with both hands and screaming in pain.

He just lay there, not moving, just staring at the woman over him.

"Mark, I just beat the shit out of a serial killer a few hours ago. When I was about to kill him, I thought of you."

"Ella, what…," he started then trailed off. He stared at his hand, caked in blood. He tried to pick himself up out of the low bush but he couldn't find any leverage. Ella did her best not to laugh. He suddenly looked a lot less threatening.

"I'm going to make this very clear," Ella said. "If you come near me, or text me, or call me, or even think of me, I'm going to tell the FBI everything about you. I'll show them the messages, the endless calls. Hell, my roommate is probably capturing this on film right now."

"Okay, Ella," Mark managed to claw back to his feet. He clutched his face, speaking to his palms. "Don't do that. That's my career."

"Should have thought of that before, shouldn't you?"

"Whatever. I'll be waiting here for you. Every day until you take me back," he shouted.

Ella knew better than to go into her apartment. It might take a few more beatings until Mark learned his lesson, and that was fine by her. She'd relish the opportunity to break his face one more time.

She backtracked down the pathway, out of the gate where the taxi was still parked. It looked like the driver had watched their altercation too.

Good, she thought. She had at least one witness.

The driver rolled the window down. "Get in," he shouted. "Damn girl, that was a good shot."

"Thanks," she jumped in the back seat. "Take me away from here please."

The car sped off, leaving Mark behind. Ella didn't look back once.

EPILOGUE

Tobias Campbell stood outside Apollo House at 3am. That was the best thing about calling on people in the middle of the night. They were always home.

Tobias hadn't killed the boy in the alleyway, just roughed him up a little. Threatened him with a broken neck, twisted a few joints, made him feel like a worthless sack of shit. But he gave him $550 for his efforts. After all, Tobias was an agent of chaos. He admired anyone who had the gall to assault someone in the middle of the day. Maybe it would inspire the young boy to commit more horrific acts throughout the state.

Killing in the middle of the street was much too risky, especially as they could have traced him back to the gambling shop. Besides, he enjoyed instilling fear. It was much more fun than the act of killing.

Fear was the great motivator and the great equalizer all in one. Fear wasn't something to be conquered; it just told you where the limits were.

That's why Agent Mia Ripley needed to experience true fear before she finally submitted to death's embrace. Doing so would tell her that she'd walked the wrong path, pursued the wrong man. She started this game by intervening in his life 20 years ago, so it was only fair that she be put through the whole spectrum of psychological torture.

As he walked up to the apartment gates, he found the entryway ajar. Some psychopaths believed that an open door was always an invitation. Ironic, considering that Miss Dark *had* invited him into her little world.

He wondered how Agent Ripley was fairing in her old age. She was a spritely thirty-something back when they first met in the middle of the woods all those years ago, but now she must be in her mid-fifties. Tobias guessed he wasn't far off the same age himself, but he didn't actually know his own age. He passed through so many foster families that all his records were lost to time. For all he knew, he could be in his hundreds. The thought amused him somewhat.

As if the invitation wasn't already clear enough, Tobias smelled something rousingly familiar in the night air. It was the scent he lived for, and one he missed greatly.

Then he spotted it. A few specks of blood along the pathway. He inspected the trail with deep curiosity, finding it led into the small bushes along the perimeter. It would have been strange, if he hadn't seen the entire thing from the shadows. It was like his walkway to the girl's apartment was already carved out. A personalized red carpet, just for him.

He reached the large glass doors and pulled on the handle.

Locked.

Not a problem. He had all this planned out long ago. His contacts had been here before him and engineered the scene to his needs.

He inspected the doorframe, the nearby walls and the lavish doormat that said *WELCOME TO APOLLO HOUSE.* He peered underneath it, then picked up the mat and inspected the underside.

There it was.

The code to the door. *4859.*

Tobias pushed the code in and heard the latch unlock. He was in, barely having to lift a finger.

The foyer was impressively grand. Marble floors, two elevators, some framed pictures of local heritage sites. What a remarkable place to live. But then again, he'd spent the past decade and a half inside a glass cage, so anything looked good by his standards.

He ascended the stairs, keeping his footsteps muffled. He remembered the door number from the time he'd sent a dead cat here. It was on the top floor, apartment number 912.

Tobias walked the whole way, glad of the length it took him. He had time to savor the environment, to think about what exactly he was going to do once he was inside the home. He'd be lying to himself if he said he hadn't spent the last few months fantasizing about it. Ever since Miss Dark had shown her pretty face in his underground chamber, he'd wanted nothing more than to rip off her head, spine still attached.

But in the confines of a private space, he had more possibilities. He could toy with her, dissect her limbs, make her eat her own tongue. The previous day when he'd sat near the river, he'd looked up at these apartments and considered hanging someone off one of the balconies. What a beautiful sight, a public suicide for all the world to see.

Did he still have the skills to talk people into it like he used to? That was his prize asset as a younger man. Convince people life was not worth living through voice alone. Of all the murders he'd committed, those were the most psychologically satisfying of all.

Unfortunately, he'd have to wait a while longer to find out. Tonight was a different approach.

Tobias walked down the carpeted hallway of the top floor, finding Miss Dark's apartment right at the end. She had a fantastic spot, very secluded, and he was sure her balcony had far reaching views into the hills.

He pulled the door handle, already knowing the result.

The door unhooked with a subtle creak, not enough to wake the sole sleeping inhabitant.

And he was among the darkness. A hardwood floor, a small table along the hallway. He waited a minute, breathed in the new air and let his eyes adjust to his surroundings. There were three doors available, two to his right and one to his left.

Before getting down to business, he decided to relish in the moment. This was what years of planning had all been for, the freedom to commit these murderous acts once more.

Tobias moved to the first door on the right. He pushed it open and found a bedroom, again steeped in blackness. It was icy cold in here, devoid of bodies. Tobias reached out, found the light switch and flicked it on.

One double bed. A wardrobe. A chest of drawers. Everything was plain and simple, and he knew that he was now standing in Miss Dark's bedroom. This was her style all over. Nondescript, plain, unobtrusive.

Tobias decided to look around. He knelt down and looked under bed, finding a bag of clothes, some decks of playing cards and a box of old photographs. He inspected them one-by-one. They were of a mustached man and a young girl.

Here it was, the reason for her being. During one of their meetings, she'd said something about her father dying at a young age. This must have been him.

It didn't matter how many cases she solved as an FBI agent, it would never bring him back to life. Maybe he could use this to talk her into suicide one day. It made for great ammunition. He imagined her terror when she came home to find the source of her nightmares sitting on her bed. It would be enough to induce instant madness.

Tobias exited the room, turned the light off and tried the next bedroom. The occupant wasn't here, just as planned.

Tobias searched the room again for anything but quickly became bored. Ella's roommate had no personality, merely embraced shallow indulgences.

He left the room as he'd found it, and lastly, made his way to the left-hand door. He pushed it open to find a lounge, lit up by a single orange lamp near the window.

There was a long television, bigger than any he'd ever seen in his life. A fancy glass coffee table, a bookshelf, two leather chairs and a small adjoining kitchen.

And the reason he came here.

The sleeping body lying on the couch.

Tobias grinned from ear to ear.

He slid into the kitchen, not making a sound. Perched on the kitchen counter was a knife rack, decked with blades in descending size.

He pulled the largest one. A glimmering silver butcher's knife, the kind he used to skin pigs once upon a time.

Tobias crept back into the living room and stood over the man. He looked a good size, fit and healthy. The kind who could probably put up a fight.

Then the man began to stir. He fidgeted with his pillow, then rolled over to show his face.

Tobias took a few deep breaths, then whispered, "Don't wake up."

The sleeping man's eyes gently opened, turning wide when they spotted the knife-wielding man over him.

His mouth fell open in a silent scream.

Oh yes, he'd missed this.

NOW AVAILABLE!

GIRL, FORSAKEN
(An Ella Dark FBI Suspense Thriller—Book 7)

FBI Special Agent Ella Dark has studied serial killers from the time she could read, devastated by the murder of her own sister, and has gained an encyclopedic knowledge of murderers. A serial killer is leaving clues around the city, using Ella's knowledge of historical murders to taunt her. Can Ella dig deep into her encyclopedic mind and crack the case? Or will this killer finally outsmart her?

"A MASTERPIECE OF THRILLER AND MYSTERY. Blake Pierce did a magnificent job developing characters with a psychological side so well described that we feel inside their minds, follow their fears and cheer for their success. Full of twists, this book will keep you awake until the turn of the last page."
--Books and Movie Reviews, Roberto Mattos (re Once Gone)

GIRL, FORSAKEN (An Ella Dark FBI Suspense Thriller) is book #7 in a long-anticipated new series by #1 bestseller and USA Today bestselling author Blake Pierce, whose bestseller Once Gone (a free download) has received over 1,000 five star reviews.

FBI Agent Ella Dark, 29, is given her big chance to achieve her life's dream: to join the Behavioral Crimes Unit. Ella's hidden obsession of gaining an encyclopedic knowledge of serial killers has led to her being singled out for her brilliant mind, and invited to join the big leagues.

Ella is confident she can solve the killer's twisted puzzle—but he always seems to be one step ahead of her.

Can she win this dangerous game of cat-and-mouse?

Or will she herself become the target?

A page-turning and harrowing crime thriller featuring a brilliant and tortured FBI agent, the ELLA DARK series is a riveting mystery, packed with suspense, twists and turns, revelations, and driven by a breakneck pace that will keep you flipping pages late into the night.

Books #8-#11 are also available!

Blake Pierce

Blake Pierce is the USA Today bestselling author of the RILEY PAGE mystery series, which includes seventeen books. Blake Pierce is also the author of the MACKENZIE WHITE mystery series, comprising fourteen books; of the AVERY BLACK mystery series, comprising six books; of the KERI LOCKE mystery series, comprising five books; of the MAKING OF RILEY PAIGE mystery series, comprising six books; of the KATE WISE mystery series, comprising seven books; of the CHLOE FINE psychological suspense mystery, comprising six books; of the JESSE HUNT psychological suspense thriller series, comprising twenty four books; of the AU PAIR psychological suspense thriller series, comprising three books; of the ZOE PRIME mystery series, comprising six books; of the ADELE SHARP mystery series, comprising fifteen books, of the EUROPEAN VOYAGE cozy mystery series, comprising four books; of the new LAURA FROST FBI suspense thriller, comprising nine books (and counting); of the new ELLA DARK FBI suspense thriller, comprising eleven books (and counting); of the A YEAR IN EUROPE cozy mystery series, comprising nine books, of the AVA GOLD mystery series, comprising six books (and counting); of the RACHEL GIFT mystery series, comprising six books (and counting); of the VALERIE LAW mystery series, comprising three books (and counting); and of the PAIGE KING mystery series, comprising three books (and counting).

An avid reader and lifelong fan of the mystery and thriller genres, Blake loves to hear from you, so please feel free to visit www.blakepierceauthor.com to learn more and stay in touch.

BOOKS BY BLAKE PIERCE

PAIGE KING MYSTERY SERIES
THE GIRL HE PINED (Book #1)
THE GIRL HE CHOSE (Book #2)
THE GIRL HE TOOK (Book #3)

VALERIE LAW MYSTERY SERIES
NO MERCY (Book #1)
NO PITY (Book #2)
NO FEAR (Book #3

RACHEL GIFT MYSTERY SERIES
HER LAST WISH (Book #1)
HER LAST CHANCE (Book #2)
HER LAST HOPE (Book #3)
HER LAST FEAR (Book #4)
HER LAST CHOICE (Book #5)
HER LAST BREATH (Book #6)

AVA GOLD MYSTERY SERIES
CITY OF PREY (Book #1)
CITY OF FEAR (Book #2)
CITY OF BONES (Book #3)
CITY OF GHOSTS (Book #4)
CITY OF DEATH (Book #5)
CITY OF VICE (Book #6)

A YEAR IN EUROPE
A MURDER IN PARIS (Book #1)
DEATH IN FLORENCE (Book #2)
VENGEANCE IN VIENNA (Book #3)
A FATALITY IN SPAIN (Book #4)

ELLA DARK FBI SUSPENSE THRILLER
GIRL, ALONE (Book #1)
GIRL, TAKEN (Book #2)
GIRL, HUNTED (Book #3)
GIRL, SILENCED (Book #4)
GIRL, VANISHED (Book 5)
GIRL ERASED (Book #6)
GIRL, FORSAKEN (Book #7)

ALMOST DEAD (Book #3)

ZOE PRIME MYSTERY SERIES
FACE OF DEATH (Book#1)
FACE OF MURDER (Book #2)
FACE OF FEAR (Book #3)
FACE OF MADNESS (Book #4)
FACE OF FURY (Book #5)
FACE OF DARKNESS (Book #6)

A JESSIE HUNT PSYCHOLOGICAL SUSPENSE SERIES
THE PERFECT WIFE (Book #1)
THE PERFECT BLOCK (Book #2)
THE PERFECT HOUSE (Book #3)
THE PERFECT SMILE (Book #4)
THE PERFECT LIE (Book #5)
THE PERFECT LOOK (Book #6)
THE PERFECT AFFAIR (Book #7)
THE PERFECT ALIBI (Book #8)
THE PERFECT NEIGHBOR (Book #9)
THE PERFECT DISGUISE (Book #10)
THE PERFECT SECRET (Book #11)
THE PERFECT FAÇADE (Book #12)
THE PERFECT IMPRESSION (Book #13)
THE PERFECT DECEIT (Book #14)
THE PERFECT MISTRESS (Book #15)
THE PERFECT IMAGE (Book #16)
THE PERFECT VEIL (Book #17)
THE PERFECT INDISCRETION (Book #18)
THE PERFECT RUMOR (Book #19)
THE PERFECT COUPLE (Book #20)
THE PERFECT MURDER (Book #21)
THE PERFECT HUSBAND (Book #22)
THE PERFECT SCANDAL (Book #23)
THE PERFECT MASK (Book #24)

CHLOE FINE PSYCHOLOGICAL SUSPENSE SERIES
NEXT DOOR (Book #1)
A NEIGHBOR'S LIE (Book #2)
CUL DE SAC (Book #3)
SILENT NEIGHBOR (Book #4)
HOMECOMING (Book #5)
TINTED WINDOWS (Book #6)